PROTECTING TEX

SEAL OF PROTECTION

SUSAN STOKER

Who does a consummate savior turn to when he finds himself in need of saving?

For years, former SEAL John "Tex" Keegan has been the literal port in every storm, saving the lives of countless men, women, and children—soldiers, sailors, and civilians—all around the world, working alone from the safety of his basement. He never expects thanks. Doesn't do it for gratitude or accolades. He's simply a protector down to his bones, doing what he was born to do, what he's always done, during and after his military career. But when someone snatches Tex off his street in broad daylight, who will come to the aid of the man who rescues all others?

The answer: *everyone*. And Lord help the people stupid enough to cross anyone *Protecting Tex...*

**Protecting Tex is a bonus book in the *SEAL of Protection* Series. It takes place several years in the future after the last book in this series and includes many characters from other series I've written over the years. When they learn Tex is in danger they all come running to help out. You can read this without having read my other books, but it'll increase your appreciation if you're familiar with some of the other characters.

A NOTE FROM THE AUTHOR

Protecting *Tex*

Who would've thought it? Tex is the man who protects everyone else. The one everyone turns to when their loved ones disappear.

The idea for this book came to me in the middle of the night and I had to think about it for quite a bit before I was ready to write. But I love how it turned out and how EVERYONE shows up to Protect Tex.

Now, you'll see a lot of old friends in this story, and you might be confused about the time line. Well, throw time line out the window! I probably got some ages wrong, and Annie's book hasn't happened yet in this story. She hasn't married Frankie and has just become a green beret.

But it's AFTER Tex has met Ryleigh (from The

Refuge series). Is that confusing? Maybe. Probably. But just go with it. No need to message or email me and tell me I messed everything up. It's fiction and I had the best time writing it.

I hope you can put your brain aside for a moment and enjoy this story for what it is…friends coming together to help one another.

Thank you all for your support and for loving Tex, Baker, Wolf, Elizabeth, Annie, Ryleigh, and ALL my characters. It means the world to me.

Now…stop reading this silly little forward…and turn the page to see what has happened and how old friends get together to find and protect Tex!

~Susan

CHAPTER 1

"What do you want for dinner tonight?"

Tex looked over at Melody and today, like every day, he was amazed she was his wife. He was well aware he wasn't the kind of guy many women would want for their partner. Mostly because he was obsessed with his job. Using his computer skills to help others. And by obsessed, he meant an entire basement filled with computers, along with electronics to build and perfect the trackers he was working to patent.

Not only that, but many people thought he was half a man because of his missing leg.

But he was also the kind of man who would drop everything to watch his daughter perform in a ballet recital. Who would adopt a girl from a war-torn country and give her a home when she had nowhere else to go. And he was a man who'd traveled across the country to meet the woman he'd only talked to online...and who'd desperately needed the kind of help he was an expert at delivering.

Tex had never imagined being as happy as he was today. He might be biased, but his wife was gorgeous. She was quite a bit older than when they'd first met, but her attractiveness hadn't diminished. She'd only gotten more beautiful in his eyes. And it had nothing to do with her looks. It was because of her generous heart. The love she had for their daughters, Akilah and Hope. Because she never griped at him when he holed up in his basement, desperately working for days to find someone who'd disappeared. His life's work had become finding those who'd gone missing—and making sure those who did the *kidnapping* were taken care of appropriately.

"John?"

Tex blinked. He'd been lost in his own head. "Sorry, Mel, what did you ask me?"

She shook her head in exasperation and repeated her question about what he wanted to eat later.

"I thought we'd decided on tacos," he said, as he

put the car in gear and backed out of the parking space at the grocery store they'd just visited.

"We did. But I was second-guessing that. Hope has volleyball practice tonight, and Akilah might come home from college for the weekend. We'll be eating late, and while tacos are easy, I thought maybe I could do something in the Crock-Pot so it'll be warm no matter when we eat."

"What about chicken and rice?" Tex asked. "It's easy to make and we have all the ingredients."

"Perfect," Melody told him with a huge smile.

Tex began driving out of the parking lot when his wife dropped a bomb on him.

"By the way, at Hope's game tomorrow night, she wants us to meet her boyfriend."

Tex slammed his foot on the brake and turned to stare at Melody incredulously. "What?"

"It's not a big deal. They're only in the seventh grade, so he's not *really* a boyfriend. They just like to hang out together and I think they've held hands a couple of times, but that's about it. She's excited about this boy, and he seems nice."

"No."

Melody chuckled. "Now, John—"

"She's too young," he said firmly. The thought of

his baby having a boyfriend made him want to throw up.

"She is," Melody agreed. "But again, she's not going to dark movie theaters with him and smooching in the back row. When she does things with him outside of school, they're in a group. Or he comes to watch her play. John, she's at that age where boys are becoming interesting, and I'm thrilled she wants us to meet him. That she's not sneaking around behind our backs about this."

A horn blared behind them and Tex looked in the rearview mirror. An angry man was shaking his fist and gesturing for him to get the hell going or move out of the way. He took a deep breath and turned his attention back to the road in front of him. As nonchalantly as he could, he asked, "What's his name?"

"Nope. Not happening," Melody told him.

"What? What's not happening?" he asked, trying to sound innocent.

"You know what I'm talking about. If I tell you this poor boy's name before you meet him, the second we get home you'll be in your basement, looking up him and his family. You'll know his parents' annual income, where they work, who their bosses are, any reprimands they've had at work, speeding tickets, and a hundred other things that are invasive as hell and completely unnecessary."

"If Hope will be spending any time with this kid, I need to know everything there is to know about him," Tex protested.

"No. You need to trust your daughter. Do you really think she'd get involved with anyone who doesn't treat her right? Every day she has the best example of how a man should act with a woman he likes. *You*, John. You've taught her by example, with everything you do for me—*and* her. You're respectful, you never raise your voice. When we disagree, we do so politely. You're supportive, kind, and you respect boundaries."

"I sound like a pussy," Tex complained under his breath.

She chuckled softly. "You're also tough, but fair. You expect Hope and Akilah to do their best at all times. You swear too much, work too hard, and both our daughters have no doubt whatsoever that if anyone dares lay a finger on them, you'll take care of them in a way that they won't ever make that mistake again. You've raised them to be smart, savvy, and strong. Trust your daughter, John."

When she put it that way, how could he do

anything *but* trust that Hope had chosen her potential boyfriend well. "Fine."

Mel chuckled again. She reached for his hand and Tex gladly gave it to her. "I love you, John. I never would've thought this would be my life when I was huddled in that hotel room in LA all those years ago."

Tex didn't like to dwell on how Melody had been running from a psycho stalker. And how that stalker had almost succeeded in taking her life. If it hadn't been for her opening up to him, letting him in and giving him the information he needed to find her—or for her coonhound, Baby—things could be much different today.

"I love you too. When we get home—"

Tex didn't get to finish his sentence. He'd just pulled onto their street when out of nowhere, a van came barreling around the bend in the road toward them. He had enough time to slam on the brakes so they didn't have a head-on collision.

Before he could get his bearings, the door of the van opened and three men dressed all in black from head to toe raced out.

"Shit, Mel, lock the door!"

But it was too late. As soon as the last word left

his mouth, his door was wrenched open and the fight was on.

Tex was hampered by the seat belt still holding him to his seat and even with adrenaline coursing through his veins, he was no match for the obviously trained men who'd ambushed him.

"Run, Mel!" he managed to say before a fist connected with his jaw and shut him up.

Before he knew what was happening, he was being dragged out of his vehicle, but he refused to give up. The fight was eerily silent, with the men who'd attacked him not saying a word.

It wasn't until he heard Melody whimpering that Tex realized she hadn't gotten away from the men who'd attacked them. "Please, whatever you want, I'll give it to you. Just don't hurt my wife."

"She'll be fine if you do what we say," one of the men said in a deep voice Tex had never heard before in his life. He had a slight accent, but Tex couldn't place it.

"Don't hurt her," he repeated. One of his eyes was swollen shut, but he could see just fine with the other one. He saw a second vehicle had pulled up behind his car while he was fighting, and as he was dragged toward the van, another man dressed all in black got behind the wheel of his vehicle.

"Hurry up, we need to get out of here," the driver of the van said impatiently, as Tex was shoved inside. He wasn't sure whether to be relieved or not when Melody was pushed in next to him. He caught her eye for a split second before he watched one of their captors pull a dark pillowcase over her head.

Then his own eyesight was cut off when he assumed another hood was shoved over his own head. The door to the van slammed shut and the driver took off, as if abducting two innocent people was an everyday occurrence for him.

Tex had been in his fair share of bad situations, but this was a hundred times worse, because he wasn't with a team of trained Navy SEALs. He was with Melody. The woman he loved more than life itself. Who he'd worked hard to keep safe since the moment they'd met. To keep evil from ever touching her again. He had no idea who the men were who'd taken them or what they wanted, but it wasn't anything good, of that he had no doubt.

No one spoke as they drove out of their neighborhood, which didn't make Tex feel all warm and fuzzy. This was planned. These guys were professionals. He tried to keep track of the turns the van took, but without sight, and thanks to what felt like frequent tight maneuvers around corners, he was quickly at a loss as to where they were going.

But he knew they'd only been driving for about ten minutes when the van slowed.

Tex tensed.

The door opened, but the van didn't fully stop. He heard Melody cry out, then scream as she was obviously pushed out of the moving vehicle.

"Mel!" he yelled, but all he got for his trouble was a fist to the gut. And the three men who'd been in the back of the van with him and Melody began to beat Tex again.

They'd handcuffed his wrists behind him before shoving him into the vehicle, and without the use of his hands, he was helpless to defend himself. By the time they stopped their assault, Tex was barely conscious.

"Why?" he managed to mumble through bleeding lips. His nose was definitely broken and he had a feeling his cheekbone was at least cracked, along with a few ribs.

"Because we can," someone said.

That was the last thing Tex remembered before he passed out.

CHAPTER 2

MELODY LAY on the ground and moaned. She hurt. Everywhere. She'd been so confused when men had rushed toward their car after getting out of the van that almost crashed into them. But as soon as John screamed at her to run, she'd acted. She had her seat belt off and her car door open even as the men were hitting John. He hadn't had a chance to fight back, and as she ran toward the large yard of a house down the street from theirs, she wondered what the hell was happening.

Unfortunately, she didn't get far. The man who'd chased her was much faster than she was in the cute little heels she'd decided to wear that morning. She regretted that decision now more than ever. He tackled her right in her neighbor's yard and she went down hard, with the weight of her pursuer on top of her.

She opened her mouth to scream, but the man anticipated that and slapped his meaty palm over her lips, muffling the sounds she made. Melody fought then, as if her life depended on getting away, but it was no use. Reinforcements had arrived and before she knew what was going on, a second man was there, helping the first to pick her up and carry her back toward the vehicles on the road.

She saw a second car had pulled up so close to their own car that the bumpers were touching. That's where the second man had obviously come from. Melody couldn't help it; a loud whimper escaped. John heard it and begged the men not to hurt her.

The next thing she knew, Melody was shoved into the van next to John. Things had happened so fast, she was still processing what was going on. But as soon as a piece of cloth was yanked over her face, terror hit hard and fast.

She'd caught John's eye before she'd been rendered blind—and what she'd seen there was fury and a promise that he'd get them both out of this. Whatever *this* was.

One of the men in the back of the van had a firm

grasp on her upper arm and was holding her so tightly, there was no way she could wrench herself out of his grip. So she decided to wait. See what happened next. At the first chance she got, Melody was going to escape. She knew better than most what happened if you were taken away from civilization…nothing good.

They drove for a short time before the van slowed. She braced herself to do something…rip the covering off her head, use her fingernails to gouge out the eyes of whoever she could reach, throw herself at the driver to make him wreck…something. *Anything.* They hadn't secured her hands behind her back, but one of the goons still firmly gripped her biceps.

She heard the door slide open but the van didn't stop. She felt the hand around her arm tighten. Then she was falling through the air after someone gave her a massive shove.

Melody had a split second to be astonished that the man had thrown her out of a moving vehicle before pain exploded in her body. She hit the pavement hard, rolling over and over.

Even through the immense pain and agony, Melody was aware that she didn't hear any sounds of John also being thrown out of the van.

Lifting a hand, she wrenched the cover off her head in time to see the back end of the white van disappearing in the distance. It was too far away to get a license plate—and as she suspected, there was no sign of John also lying anywhere nearby after being thrown out of the van.

She sat on the ground for a moment, trying to understand what the hell just happened. Nothing made sense. The men hadn't even touched her, not really. She hadn't been bound, hadn't been hurt too badly as she was being subdued.

Of course, *now* she was injured. Her left hip was throbbing where she'd landed on it. Her head too. She felt blood dripping down the back of her neck. Her left arm was screaming, and when Melody looked down, she saw it was bent in an awkward angle, obviously broken.

She was covered in road rash and her shoes were long gone…she probably lost them in the struggle in her neighbor's yard. How in the world could they have been kidnapped in the middle of the day, and not one person saw it happen? But then again, maybe someone *did* see it happen and they'd called the police. The cops could be looking for them even now, fanning out across the town of Washington, Pennsylvania, in search of her and John.

Looking around, Melody realized she had no idea where she was. She was lying half on and half off the road in the tall grass. There was a fence behind her and large fields on either side of the road, with some kind of crop growing.

Frowning, she looked back the way they came. There were no cars. No sounds. Her kidnappers had pushed her out of the van in the middle of nowhere. She'd lived in the area a long time, but she didn't recognize the area she was in now. Tears threatened, but Melody forced them back. She couldn't cry. Not now. Not when the men who'd taken her still had John. He was a badass former Navy SEAL, yes, but she couldn't get the vision of his already bruised face out of her mind. He was bleeding, and she'd seen cuffs on his wrists before that cover had been put over her head.

It struck Melody then that they'd probably taken her to keep John compliant. And it had worked.

She needed to get help.

She tried to stand, and found it was almost impossible. Her hip joint felt as if it was out of its socket, and her arm hurt so bad, her vision went black when it moved as she struggled to her feet. She stood in the road weaving, praying she wouldn't fall and hurt herself even more than she already was.

Determination filled her. She was the only link to John. She tried to remember every detail of what had just happened. What the van looked like, how the men sounded—even though they hadn't spoken very much—even smells at this point. Any information the police might be able to use.

Melody began to slowly limp down the road, praying she'd see a house before the pain became too much and she passed out. She'd only hobbled about five steps or so before she saw something in the road up ahead that definitely looked out of place.

It was a brick that had been painted yellow. As she got closer, Melody saw there was a piece of paper wrapped around it, secured with a rubber band. It had to have been thrown out of the van along with her. Why else would it be here?

She wasn't John "Tex" Keegan's wife for nothing, Melody knew better than to touch either the brick or the note with her bare hands. She prayed their kidnappers had left fingerprints or some kind of touch DNA on either the paper or the brick.

Desperately wanting to know what the hell was written on that paper, Melody kept walking. She'd send the police back to pick it up. Now that she was upright, she had a feeling if she stopped, she might not be able to get started again. Every step was excruciatingly painful. But she'd suffer any amount of discomfort if it meant getting help for John.

The thought of what he might be going through was almost enough to break her, but Melody took a deep breath and kept walking, looking behind her every now and then, terrified her kidnappers would decide they'd made a mistake in letting her go and come back to find her.

She had no idea how long she'd been walking, as time had no meaning through the agony coursing through her body, when she saw a car in the distance coming toward her.

Stopping, Melody moved to the middle of the road. The car would either have to run her over or stop. And if it was her kidnappers coming back, they'd surely choose the former. But she was at the end of her rope. She couldn't take one more step.

To her immense relief, the car slowed as it got close. A woman was driving, and Melody could see two young children in car seats in the back.

The woman stopped and stared at Melody in shock.

Melody didn't move. She didn't want to seem like a threat, especially to a mom with kids. The sight of the children made Melody think of her own. She was suddenly so damn thankful that Hope hadn't been with them. That she'd been spared this experience.

"Please," she said, raising her voice in the hopes she could be heard through the closed windows of the car and over the engine. "I need help." Melody even held her good arm out from her side, trying to show she was unarmed.

The woman rolled the driver's-side window down an inch or two. "I'm calling the police!" she yelled.

Melody nodded, relief making her dizzy. Or maybe that was the pain of being shoved out of a moving vehicle. She didn't dare move out of the middle of the road though, petrified the woman would simply drive away and not do as she'd promised...namely call the police.

She watched as the woman brought a phone up to her ear and her lips moved. Melody held eye contact with her savior, not wanting to risk looking away for fear she was an illusion. A mirage. Made up in Melody's pain-filled mind.

Eventually, the woman cautiously opened the car door and stood by it with the phone up to her ear. "Nine-one-one wants to know what's wrong," she called out.

Melody wanted to collapse. Wanted to give in to

the unconsciousness hovering at the edges of her mind. But she forced herself to stay upright. Aware. John needed her. "My husband and I were kidnapped. They pushed me out of the van, but they still have him. Please, he needs help!"

"What's your name?" The woman's voice was gentler now. She even took a step away from the car.

"Melody Keegan. My husband's name is John. We live in Washington. It was a white van. There were three men—no...that's how many were in the van. I think there were five or six total. Shoot. I'm not one hundred percent sure how many there were."

The woman walked closer to Melody. She was still talking to the 9-1-1 operator, relaying the information Melody had given her, then adding, "She looks hurt bad. She's bleeding and her arm doesn't look right. Please hurry."

"Thank you," Melody whispered, more than grateful that this woman had gone out of her way to help. It occurred to her that she could've easily swerved around her in the road. She wasn't actually in any condition to force the woman to stop.

"Do you want to sit?" the woman asked, gesturing toward the side of the road.

Melody shook her head. She wanted a lot of things

right that moment, but sitting wasn't one of them. She wanted John. For the first time, dread filled her. She had no idea how to live without him. He'd been her rock for so long. He had to be all right. He *had* to.

Her husband was the strongest man she knew. He'd be fine. Soon, this would be nothing but a bad memory. He'd be back in his basement scouring the internet and dark web for intel and helping to find those who needed him the most.

The irony that *John* was the one who needed to be found right now wasn't lost on her. He didn't have a tracker; that she knew. Besides, she had no idea how to work the software on his computers, even if he *was* wearing one. She could surf the web, shop, do email, social media, and chat rooms, but that was about it.

It hit Melody then that if the police couldn't track her husband down in a few hours, she'd need to call in reinforcements. John had a huge circle of friends and acquaintances. People he'd helped in the past. People who she hoped wouldn't hesitate to return the favor. She had no idea how to get a hold of the people John knew, but she knew who to start with.

Wolf. Matthew Steel. One of his oldest and

dearest friends. Matthew and his SEAL teammates, all retired now, would know what to do.

By the time Melody heard sirens in the distance, the pain coursing through her veins had overpowered almost everything else.

One more minute. That's all you need to endure. Stay conscious one more minute. Just long enough to tell the police about the brick. To warn them about DNA and fingerprints. Then you can close your eyes and sleep.

No, you can't sleep. You need to tell them what happened.

Two more minutes then. That's all. You can do this. You have to stay awake, Hope will be worried when she gets home and you aren't there. You have to suck it up, Mel. Call Amy, ask her to come look after Hope if you don't get home in time. Oh! The groceries! They'll go bad if they aren't put away. She can do that too...

Melody was aware her thoughts were ricocheting from one topic to another. But it was the only way she could keep her mind off the agony that was getting worse every second. As the adrenaline waned from her system, the pain was almost overwhelming.

She had to get the cops to contact her best friend. Amy Smith. Ames. She'd take care of Hope. The groceries. Her car. Call Akilah and let her know what was going on. All of it.

Remaining on her feet as the ambulance and police car pulled up was torture. She waited for them to come to her. As soon as they got close, she began to speak. Tell them everything swirling around in her brain. Because she had a feeling as soon as the medics began to work on her, the pain would be too much and she wouldn't be able to stay conscious. Even if she did, the painkillers she hoped like hell they'd give her would put her in a fog.

She had one chance to tell them as much info as possible so they could find John. She wasn't going to let him down. No way in hell.

CHAPTER 3

WHEN TEX REGAINED CONSCIOUSNESS, he realized a few things simultaneously.

One, he was naked. He'd been stripped of all his clothes, even his underwear.

Two, the bastards had taken his prosthetic, as well. The only way he was getting out of wherever he was being held was by hopping—which pissed him off.

Three, it was fucking dark as hell.

And four, there was heavy metal music playing so loudly, there was no way he could hear anyone talking even if they were standing right in front of him.

Putting his hands out, Tex tried to understand where he was. He crawled as best he could, attempting to get to a wall, or window, or something. But there was no window. No furniture. Nothing. He quickly realized he was in a box of some sort. Based on his height and that his head and feet didn't touch the ends of the box it was in when he was lying on his back, but if he put his arms over his head he could feel the wall above him, he figured the space he was in was about seven feet long by three feet wide. He couldn't stand up, but at least it wasn't a fucking coffin. He could get on his knee and stretch. He estimated it was about five feet tall.

That was it. All the intel he had about his current situation. No idea about who had taken him, what they wanted, or where Melody was. It was that last one that ate at Tex. Had she gotten hurt when they'd pushed her out of the van?

He scoffed. What a dumb question. Of *course* she'd been hurt. She'd been pushed out of a moving fucking vehicle!

Tex had been held captive before while a SEAL. He dealt with people who'd been kidnapped on a daily basis. But this felt different...and not because it was *him* in this fucking box. Unease swam through his veins. He had no information. Nothing to go on to try to figure out who'd taken him and why. No one had said much of anything when they'd been beating him. It was his experience that human nature led kidnappers to spout off, to air their grievances when they took someone, or at least after they had them under control. The fact that whoever had taken him hadn't was...worrisome.

"Hey!" he yelled, hoping to get someone's attention. It was a risk, because if they knew he was awake, they could decide to hurt him some more. But the more they interacted with him, the more information he'd hopefully have to use against them.

He barely heard himself over the sound of the music. He tried again.

"Is anyone there?" he yelled.

Nothing. He got no response. No one came to see what he was hollering about.

Using his hands to feel his way around the box, he found what he thought was a door of sorts, but there was no knob on his side. No lock to pick. He was well and truly stuck.

Sighing, Tex leaned against the back of the box and racked his mind to try to figure out who'd have the balls to kidnap him and his wife in the middle of the day. On their own residential street, at that. No one came to mind.

Yes, Tex dealt with a lot of assholes in his line of work. People he had to have pissed off because he'd foiled whatever nefarious plan they'd had. He snooped into personal financial records and exposed secrets bad guys would rather never see the light of day. But he wasn't an idiot. He knew how to cover his tracks. He left no trace of his presence when he ferreted out information online. Besides, there weren't many people who'd know what to look for anyway.

He'd never charged anyone for finding people. That was simply the decent fucking thing to do. But he *did* charge for his trackers—and as a result, Tex had made a fortune over the years. They became more and more popular over the years, and were now standard in the special forces communities he served. The government paid a pretty penny for exclusive rights to the technology he'd created.

Of course, right about now, he could've used one of his newest subcutaneous trackers, himself. But even though he busted bad guys all the time, foiled their plans by finding people they kidnapped, he honestly didn't think *he'd* be a target for kidnapping himself. Which was incredibly stupid on his part. His life these days was boring as hell…and he loved every second. He spent the days in his basement, tinkering with the trackers and searching for the missing, and his evenings with his wife and daughter. The past several years had been idyllic. Watching Akilah grow up and become more and more comfortable in her own skin. Seeing Melody blossom as a mother. And of course, doting on his baby, Hope.

Hell, the toughest time he'd had in recent memory was when their coonhound, Baby, had died. She'd lived a long life, being spoiled shamelessly. He and Melody had talked about getting another dog, but decided against it. No other dog could live up to Baby, and it wouldn't be fair to another animal to constantly be compared to the best dog that had ever lived.

Tex rubbed his head. It fucking hurt. The bastards who'd taken him hadn't pulled any punches —literally—when they were beating him. His nose felt broken and every inch of his face was swollen and sore. His ribs were bruised at best, cracked or broken at worst. He probably had bruises all over his body...but he was alive. And as he always told people, being alive meant a chance to escape and be rescued. He just had to be patient. His captors would mess up; they always did.

But the niggling worry in the back of his mind was...who would be able to ferret out the mistakes they made. Usually that person was *him*. He could find a specific needle in a stack of needles. He wasn't as confident in the detectives on the local police force. Oh, they were good. But Tex was the best. And he had a feeling the men who'd taken him were being paid very well to not make any mistakes. Which didn't bode well for him.

"Fuck me," Tex said, not able to hear his own words because of the music thumping all around him.

There were people who were almost as good as him. One, he could think of who had skills better than his. If they all worked together, they were definitely better than he'd ever be. But would they be contacted? If Melody was hurt too badly, she'd probably be in the hospital and in no condition to seek out anyone. It could be days before his closest friends realized he was missing. Days he might not have to spare.

"Shit," he said out loud. He had no idea how much time had passed since he'd been yanked off the street, but it wasn't good that he was already getting depressed and maudlin. "Snap out of it, Tex," he told himself. "Melody is smart. And strong as hell. She's got this."

He had so many questions swirling around in his

head, but Melody's capability wasn't one of them. He trusted his wife implicitly.

A small grin formed on his lips. If he knew Mel, she was raising hell and telling the cops how to do their job. She'd been Tex's wife a long time. Some of what he did *had* to have rubbed off on her. She'd get the ball rolling on the investigation, of that he had no doubt. His Mel would move heaven and earth to find him. If she couldn't do it herself, she'd contact those who could.

Thinking about his wife was both painful and a balm to his wounded soul. He prayed she was all right physically and wasn't even now in the hands of the same people who'd locked him away. He'd heard her get pushed out of that van, but that didn't mean someone else hadn't picked her up and taken her to a different location.

That thought made Tex want to puke. He knew all too well what usually happened to women in captivity. But he doubted the men who'd taken him had passed her on to another group of kidnappers by pushing her out of a car. No, they would've brought her to a warehouse somewhere and made a much less dramatic—and public—handoff.

The men who ambushed them on their way home from the store wanted only him. For what end, he'd yet to figure out. But he would. And they'd pay. One way or another, they'd fucking pay.

MELODY HURT.

All over.

But the pain was secondary to the anxiety coursing through her veins. The police kept asking the same questions over and over again. She wasn't sure they even believed her outlandish story about what had happened.

She begged them to go to her neighbors and ask about security cameras. Surely there was *someone* who'd caught some of their kidnapping on tape.

Was that what it was even called these days? "On tape?" No, there was no more tape. On film? There wasn't film either.

Fuck, her mind kept wandering off into random topics. She needed to focus. And she needed a phone. She had no idea where her own cell was. Still in their car, probably.

"Did you find our car?" she asked.

"Of course. It was in your driveway," the detective who was sitting next to her hospital bed said calmly.

Melody blinked. "What?"

"Your driveway. That's where we found your car."

"Did you fingerprint it?"

The detective stared at her without saying a word for the longest time.

"I *told* you, we were yanked out of our car in the middle of the road. If our car was in our driveway, someone drove it there. Someone who wasn't me or John. They might've left fingerprints. I realize it's a long shot because they seemed really organized and like they had their shit together, but maybe."

"We're having the car towed. Forensics will go over it with a fine-tooth comb."

Melody nodded, relieved.

"We're doing our best to be on the lookout for your husband, and the van, but without a better description than 'a white van,' I'm not sure how successful we'll be."

Melody hated to hear that, but she wasn't surprised. "They put that hood over my head before I could see the license plate. Did you find it? The hood, I mean?"

The detective nodded.

"Good. And the yellow brick? That too?"

"Yes."

"What'd the note say?"

"I'm not sure. It will be reviewed by forensics as well. Good job on not touching it. Now, what can you tell me about your relationship with your husband?"

Melody blinked. "My relationship?"

She hated that she was repeating his questions, but that one was so out of left field, she wasn't sure she understood why he was asking. But then again, she did have a concussion where she'd hit her head on the pavement while she was rolling over and over after being pushed out of a fucking moving vehicle, so she couldn't be too hard on herself.

"Yeah. Are you getting along? Do you have money issues? Are either one of you having an affair?"

Melody was so surprised, she could only stare at the detective in confusion. "What would any of *that* have to do with us getting kidnapped? Shouldn't you be asking me if John has any enemies? If I know of anyone who might want to abduct him? Hurt him?"

"Do you?"

The suspicious tone of the man's voice clued Melody in for the first time that he thought *she* had something to do with what happened.

Leaning forward in the hospital bed, she winced, but met the detective's gaze. "I will say this once, and then I expect you to do your damn job and find my husband before the men who took him can hurt him —or worse. I. Had. Nothing. To. Do. With. This. Absolutely *nothing*. The only thing I want is my husband back."

"I want that too. But I need information in order to find him."

Melody sat back, annoyed beyond belief. "I need my phone," she blurted. She wasn't going to get anywhere with this guy. She understood that now. So she needed help.

"It's at the station. You'll get it back after we get a warrant and can look through it."

That was the last straw. Her head hurt. Her arm was in agony, and she wasn't looking forward to a cast being put on it—she'd been waiting for the doctor to do just that when the detective asked to speak with her. Her hip was screaming. Not to mention the road rash she had on the entire left side of her body felt as if she'd had her skin peeled off slowly and painfully...because she had.

"John and I are more in love today than we were when we got married, if that's possible. No, we have no money issues, and neither of us is having an affair. I need the numbers in my phone so I can make some calls."

"Does John have life insurance?"

That was it. Melody was definitely done now.

"Get out," she hissed. "I'm ending this interrogation. I'm assuming I'm not under arrest, so I'm done talking to you. If you get your head out of your ass, let me know and I'll be happy to talk to you again. Treating me like a suspect instead of someone who was fucking kidnapped and pushed out of a goddamn car is asinine, and it isn't getting you anywhere near finding my husband."

"Mel!"

The shout from Melody's best friend, Amy, at the doorway was the sweetest sound Melody had heard in hours. "Ames!"

The devastated look on her friend's face told Melody all she needed to know about what she looked like. Amy pushed past the detective—who'd stood up to back away—and leaned over the hospital bed. She very carefully hugged Melody, and even though it hurt, nothing had also felt so good.

"If you remember anything else, please give me a call," the detective said. "I'll leave my card here on the table."

"How can I call you? You have my phone, remember?" Melody said snarkily.

The detective simply nodded at her and Amy, then left the room.

"Wait, he's leaving? What about security? Bodyguards? The assholes who did this could come back and take you again!" Amy exclaimed.

"They pushed me out of a moving van, Ames. I don't think they want me."

"But what if they do?" she countered. "What if they were just torturing you or something?"

Melody didn't even want to think about that. "Did you see Hope?" She'd asked the hospital personnel to contact Amy and request she check on her daughter. The last thing she needed was Hope to have been abducted as well.

"I did. She's good. She's at the school for volleyball practice. I told her that you'd been in an accident but were okay. That you told me to tell her to stay at school. I also talked to her coach briefly and explained what happened. She said she'd watch Hope like a hawk to make sure nothing happened to her. I'll go to the school after her practice is over and I'll bring her here, so you can explain what happened. Then she can go home with you."

"Thanks," Melody said, relieved beyond measure that she had such an amazing friend to rely on. She didn't want to even think about Hope being in the hands of the same people who'd taken her and John, and she felt much better that someone was keeping an eye on her.

"Now, what's going on with finding John?"

"The detective wanted to know if either of us was having an affair and if John had life insurance...insinuating that I had something to do with this. I need my phone, Amy. At least the numbers in it. I need to call some of John's friends. He needs them."

Amy looked pissed beyond belief. "That fucking asshole! You and John are as solid as anyone I've ever met. Where's your phone?"

"At the police station."

Amy winced. "Shit. I don't suppose that detective was leaving to go get it and bring it to you."

Melody shook her head, ignoring the pain it caused.

"Right. So...you got a new phone last year, right? What'd you do with your old one?"

"I think it's in the junk drawer in our kitchen. I told John we should erase all the data and sell it, but he said that wiping it never really works and the data can still be downloaded if someone knows how to do it." She didn't really mind talking about John. It was painful, but also a comfort right about now. He was probably more worried about *her* than whatever was happening to himself.

"Perfect. I'll go get it. It's probably dead, but I'll charge it on my way back here. It's probably still got your contacts and stuff on there, right?"

Melody perked up. "Yeah. You're a genius!"

To her shock, tears filled Amy's eyes. "I'm so glad you're all right. I was so scared when you called and told me what happened. I know it sucks that you were hurt, but I'm so glad they didn't take you too."

"They only took me to keep John compliant," Melody whispered, more sure of that than anything else. "He was fighting them hard, but as soon as he saw that they had me, he gave up. Went with them without further hassle."

"Shit."

"Yeah."

"Do you have any idea who took him?"

"None."

"Right. You need your phone. I'll be right back."

"Thanks, Amy."

"No need to thank me."

"Now you sound like John."

Amy's lips twitched. "That's because I've been around him almost as much as I've been around you. Hashtag best friends for life," she said, using the silly words they'd said since meeting each other as schoolgirls. It was actually one of the things that had pissed off Melody's stalker all those years ago, but both women had refused to stop using the phrase.

"Hashtag love you," Melody whispered, feeling exhausted all of a sudden.

"Tell the doc that he better be gentle with you, or he'll have me to answer to," Amy said fiercely. Then she squeezed Melody's good hand briefly and hurried out of the room.

Melody closed her eyes. She wasn't strong enough for this. John always praised her as being one of the strongest women he knew, but she wasn't. Not really. All she wanted to do was close her eyes and sleep, block out everything that had happened. But she couldn't do that. Neither she nor John could rely on the local cops. They'd do their best, of that she had no doubt, but if they were thinking *she* had anything to do with his disappearance, they were so off base it wasn't funny. And it would take too much time for them to figure out that she was completely innocent and get back on the trail of the real kidnappers. Time John didn't have.

He was in trouble. How she knew that, Melody wasn't sure. Maybe it was because of how professional their kidnappers seemed. How smooth the abduction had been. If John was going to be found, alive, he needed the best of the best looking for him. And while she didn't know who those people were, Wolf would. John's best friend had insider information Melody didn't have on the people John had worked with in the past. The former Navy SEAL would know who to call, how to get the ball rolling to find his friend.

She was counting on it.

CHAPTER 4

THE DOOR to Tex's prison opened suddenly, letting in a shaft of light that was so painful, he involuntarily slammed his eyes closed to protect his vision. In that split second, his arms were grabbed and he was yanked to his foot. The music was suddenly cut off and the silence that followed was so blissful, Tex almost didn't care that he was naked and bruised and being dragged harshly out of that damn box.

Squinting, trying to get his eyes to adjust to the sudden influx of light, Tex saw he was in a room with absolutely no furniture except for a single wooden chair...which didn't bode well for him.

Sure enough, he was slammed down onto the seat, his hands wrenched behind him. They were tied, too tightly, and only then did the two men back away.

They made the mistake of not tying his one leg to the chair as well, but it was too early in this game to show his hand. If they thought he was completely helpless without his prosthetic, that might be their one fatal misstep. For now, he needed intel. Needed to know who had taken him and why.

"Who are you?" He figured he might as well ask. Maybe he'd get lucky and they'd tell him what he needed to know without too much digging.

In response, the taller of the two men stepped forward and slammed a meaty fist into Tex's jaw.

Fuck. Okay, maybe they weren't going to tell him anything.

The men took turns punching him in the face, the stomach, kicking him…doing as much damage as they could with their fists. Tex did his best to protect his vital organs by tightening his core, and to avoid getting his jaw broken, but he wasn't so sure he was successful in the latter.

Instead of concentrating on the pain his captors were inflicting, Tex did his best to memorize anything he could about both men. They were tall and muscular. Both had dark brown hair and brown eyes. They were wearing black handkerchiefs over their mouths and noses.

The shorter man, who was around Tex's height, six feet or so, was more muscular than his companion. He was sweating profusely and smelled like fried food. He had dirt under his fingernails and grease stains on his hands. He was also wearing a wedding band.

The taller one, who was about six foot three, wore a short-sleeve shirt that allowed Tex to see a tattoo on his forearm. To his surprise and disbelief, it was the SEAL trident. An eagle holding a trident, a symbol any Navy SEAL would recognize anywhere.

So much for brotherhood, Tex thought, as he slouched in the chair, pain making it impossible to hold his head up anymore. Throughout the beating, neither man spoke. Not giving Tex any clues to their nationality or what part of the country they might be from. He had no idea if he knew these men, if they'd crossed paths before. Had Tex worked with the taller guy? Had he tracked his SEAL team when they were on a mission?

When the smaller guy released his hands, Tex literally fell onto the floor. Everything hurt. Blood dripped from his lip and nose, and he had a whole new set of bruises covering the ones they'd made when they'd kidnapped him in the first place.

He saw a foot swing out from the corner of his eye and found the strength to roll abruptly to the side, avoiding taking the steel-toed boot to the head.

The large man who'd tried to kick him laughed. It was a sinister sound. One without mercy or remorse.

"Back to your cage, asshole," the man growled. "Start crawling."

Tex did as he was ordered. If the men thought to humiliate him by taking his clothes and making him crawl on the floor, they'd fail. Tex's only mission was to survive another day. To get back to his family. Nothing else mattered. He'd do whatever he was told as soon as he was told to do it, if it meant getting back to Mel. He had every confidence that his wife would know what to do to find him. She'd never give up. Ever. That was his woman. Strong as hell.

When Tex made it back to the box, he saw that at some point while he was getting beaten, someone had put a bottle of water in his makeshift cell. That was all he saw before the door slammed shut behind him and the damn music was turned back on.

It seemed even darker in the box now than

before. Tex crawled to where he'd seen the water and it took way more time to open that simple bottle than he would've thought possible. Tex had the thought that the water could be drugged, but at this point, he didn't care. He needed it. Again, if he was going to get back to Melody, Hope, and Akilah, he'd do whatever he had to in order to survive.

His stomach cramped as the water hit it, wanting more substance than the precious liquid could offer, but Tex blocked any thoughts of hunger from his mind. This most likely wasn't going to be a short stay in the box. The men who'd taken him were good. Too good.

But they didn't know some of the people Tex worked with. As soon as they got wind of what was going on, they'd find him. He had no doubt whatsoever of that. And when they did…they'd rain hellfire down on his kidnappers.

MELODY'S ARM itched from the drying plaster used to make the cast on her arm. But she didn't care. Amy had returned from the house with her old phone and thankfully all the contacts were there. Including Matthew Steel's. Wolf. She'd wanted to call him as soon as she got his number, but the doctor had decided to discharge her. So there'd been forms to sign and scrubs to put on, since the clothes she'd been wearing when she and John were abducted were bloody and torn, and the detective had taken them as "evidence."

It was laughable that the man thought she had something to do with this. But then again, he saw the worst in humanity day in and day out. What was the statistic? Over forty percent of murdered married women were killed by their husbands? She wasn't sure what the numbers were for wives killing their husbands, but obviously the detective had to look at those who were close to John for answers.

But he wouldn't find any skeletons in Melody's closet. Whoever had done this was someone obscure. Who had a beef against her husband.

Amy drove like a bat out of hell on the way to Melody's house. She wasn't happy Melody wanted to go back there, but she couldn't think of anywhere she'd rather be than somewhere she was surrounded by happy memories of John. Everywhere she looked in their home, she'd be reminded of him. Of better times.

"I think I should stay here with you," Amy said, after she finished walking through the house with a shovel she'd grabbed that was leaning against the side of the house. John had planted a new tree the other day and hadn't put it back in the garage yet. Melody would've laughed at the sight of her best friend menacingly brandishing the shovel as she opened each and every door in the house, but there was nothing remotely funny about the situation.

"Someone needs to pick up Hope," Melody told her.

"I can have my husband do it. He had an important meeting today, but it should be over by now. Maybe. Or I could text her and have her get a ride home."

"Please, Ames. I trust *you* with her. She's going to have questions. She's not stupid. You can bring her right back here and I'll tell her what I know...which isn't a hell of a lot. You can stay the night. Your husband too. In fact, I'd feel better if you did. But I need a moment to call one of John's friends. I need help. *He* needs help. Now."

Amy sighed. "All right. But I'm setting the alarm when I leave."

Melody nodded, perfectly all right with that.

Amy came over to the couch, where she'd plunked Melody when they'd entered, and hugged her once more. "You scared me," she whispered as she held on tightly. "I swear my heart stopped when you said you'd been kidnapped."

"I know," Melody replied. "I'm sorry."

"Don't be sorry!" Amy said almost violently. "It wasn't your fault. And if you had called anyone else, I would've been pissed. Okay, I'm going so I can return quickly. Are you sure you'll be okay by yourself until I get back?"

Melody nodded. She *was* a little nervous to be alone, but as soon as Amy was gone she'd have Matthew on the other end of the phone line. If anything happened, he'd know. Which wouldn't help her a whole hell of a lot, but she didn't want to wait one second longer than necessary to get someone more capable than her, or the damn detective, looking into where the hell those men had taken John, and why.

Taking a deep breath once she heard Amy's car back out of the driveway, Melody reached for her phone. It wasn't activated for cell service, but she could use the wi-fi calling on it. She clicked Matthew's name in her contact list and held her breath as she waited for him to answer.

Her heart was beating way too fast, and she had no idea why.

"Hello?"

"Matthew?"

"Yeah. Melody? What's up?"

He had to be wondering why she was calling him. Melody had called Caroline many times over the years. But she couldn't remember contacting her husband once. "I need help. No, *John* needs help. He's been taken."

"*What*? Taken?"

"Yeah." It didn't take her long to recount the day's events.

"Fuck. Are you all right?"

"I will be. My arm is broken, and I have a concussion and road rash from hell. But I'm all right. It's John I'm worried about."

"Right. What do the cops say?"

"The detective thinks I had something to do with it."

The disgusted huff of breath Matthew let out made Melody feel a hundred times better. "Then he's an idiot."

Amazingly, Melody found herself defending the guy. "He doesn't know us from Adam. For all he knows, I hired someone, or several someones, to do this and to let me go."

"To push you from a moving vehicle? Not a chance in hell."

"Anyway, I know John has worked with some people who are good at computers. Who do what he does. But I don't know their names. He keeps that part of his life completely separate because he wants to protect me from the horrors I know he deals with all the time. I keep telling him that I can handle anything he wants to talk to me about, but he's stubborn and doesn't want to burden me with his work details. Do you know anyone who might be able to look into this? Might be able to help? I don't know... maybe someone John has worked with in the past, or communicated with, or whatever. But someone who can perhaps hack into his computer? I don't know if that's even possible, because we're talking about John here, but I also don't know how else to figure this out."

"I know who to call," Matthew said in a voice so calm and reassuring, Melody instantly relaxed...and tears formed in her eyes.

"But I doubt anyone is gonna be able to hack remotely into his computer. There's no way in hell Tex would leave a crack of any kind in his system. The people I'm going to call, they might need to be there in person. Is that okay?"

"Of course. I'd welcome anyone and everyone

who can help," Melody reassured John's oldest friend.

"Good. And Caroline and I will be on the red-eye out your way tonight as well."

"You don't have to—"

"Bullshit. We're coming. How's Hope? Does Akilah know?"

Just knowing help was on the way made Melody almost lose her composure. She wiped the errant tears off her cheeks and sniffed discreetly. "Amy is picking Hope up from volleyball practice now. I'll call Akilah after I talk to her sister."

"All right. And you're not alone?"

"Well, right this second, I am. But I'm sure Amy's already called her husband, even though I told her I'd be fine, and he's probably on his way over here. And she'll be back with Hope. And Amy and her husband are both spending the night."

"I don't love that you're alone right now, but at least tell me the doors and windows are locked."

"Of course they are."

"Good. What else can you tell me about what happened today?"

The fact that Matthew was all business made it easier to talk about what happened. "There was a yellow brick with a note tied around it on the ground, near where I was pushed out of the van. I didn't touch it because I didn't want to mess with any DNA or fingerprints that might be on it. I have no idea what it said. Do you think it could be a ransom note? If so, why haven't the police contacted me about it?"

"I don't know. But I guarantee before the night's over, we'll know what it said. As soon as I make some phone calls, Tex's friends will be on that shit. We'll let you know as soon as we find out. Okay?"

Melody's eyes began to leak once more. The unconditional support Matthew was giving her felt amazing after the detective's suspicions.

"Will you be okay while I make arrangements for us to get to you?"

"Yes."

"Good. And, Melody?"

"Yeah?"

"Tex is the toughest bastard I know. If anyone can make it through this, it's him. Okay?"

"Yeah. But what if they want to kill him?" Melody whispered, speaking aloud her greatest fear for the first time.

"If they wanted to kill him, they would've done that on the street," Matthew said as gently as he could. "They would've put a bullet in his head right there in the driver's seat of his car. They took him for a reason. Maybe they're making a point, maybe they want money, maybe they want revenge. I have no idea. But his friends will figure it out, and we'll make every single person who had a hand in this pays. They'll regret laying one finger on Tex *and* you."

By the time Matthew was finished speaking, his tone was deathly hard. It was a tone Melody had never heard from him before. And instead of freaking her out, it was reassuring. And he was right. The men who'd taken them must want John for a reason. His friends just needed to figure out why, and who, and then find where he'd been taken.

"Melody? You hear me?"

"I hear you."

"Good. Stay safe. We'll be there in the morning. But rest assured the people I call will be on this the second I tell them Tex is missing."

"Okay."

"Okay. Love you, sweetie."

"Love you too. See you soon."

"Soon," Matthew parroted.

CHAPTER 5

IT TOOK Wolf several moments after he hung up to calm down. Tex was missing. Had been *kidnapped*. If he hadn't just talked to Melody and heard the terror in her voice, he would've thought someone was fucking with him.

Tex didn't get kidnapped. He was the man who found those who were.

The one question front and center in Wolf's mind was…who? Who hated Tex so much that they'd go to these lengths to get to him?

Pulling his laptop closer, he quickly reserved two red-eye tickets out of San Diego to Pittsburgh. They cost a fortune, but Wolf didn't even hesitate to click the purchase button. His closest friend was missing. He'd pay whatever it cost to get to Melody's side.

The next step was calling Elizabeth Turner. It was interesting how life came full circle. Beth had been kidnapped by a serial killer. along with his friend Summer, up in Big Bear quite a few years ago. She'd moved to San Antonio, Texas, to deal with the aftermath, where she'd met a firefighter named Cade. He'd helped her overcome her agoraphobia and, in the process, she'd been introduced to Tex.

Turned out Beth was one hell of a hacker. She and Tex became fast friends, and last Wolf heard, she continued to work with Tex from time to time. He hoped that was still the case.

He didn't beat around the bush when she answered. "Beth? This is Wolf...Matthew Steel. I'm married to Caroline?"

"Of course. How are you?" Beth asked, the curiosity as to why he was calling easy to hear in her voice.

"I'm sorry this isn't a social call. Tex has been kidnapped." Wolf decided delivering the news like ripping off a Band-Aid was best.

Dead silence followed his statement.

"Beth? Did you hear me?"

"I heard you, but I'm not sure I believe it," she said.

Wolf proceeded to relay all the information

53

Melody had shared with him about what happened. "Caroline and I are on our way to Pennsylvania tonight to be with Melody and see if we can be of any help. But what Tex really needs is someone like *him*. Someone who can get intel. And you were the first person I thought of."

"Holy shit. Tex kidnapped. I'm having a hard time wrapping my head around this. But yes, of *course* I'll help. But honestly, a better person than me with the dark web is a woman named Ryleigh. She lives in New Mexico. Tex recently met her, and he told me that she's even more talented than *him* when it came to hacking and getting into places that are supposedly secure."

"That's right! I know her! I met her not too long ago myself, when some shit went down at the resort where she works. Caroline and I were actually there. I'd forgotten that Tex said something about her being a computer genius."

"Do you want me to contact her?" Beth asked.

"No. I'm on it. I need you to start searching. See if you can find anyone who has a grudge against Tex. Who might've been posting shit online about him. We need any and all information about anyone who could be behind this."

"On it," Beth said. "Would you mind if Cade and I came to Pennsylvania too?"

"You'd be okay with that? I mean…no offense, but I know about your condition," Wolf said as gently as he could.

"I'm good. I mean, I'm not saying I want to go hang out at a Pittsburgh Steelers game or anything, but as long as Cade's with me and I'm on my meds, I can handle it. I've come a long way since those awful days after I first moved here."

"From what I've heard, you've done an amazing job. I'll send you Melody and Tex's address. And you'll have my number so you can keep in touch."

Beth chuckled. "No need. I can find both on my own."

Wolf had forgotten who he was dealing with for a moment. "Of course you can. All right, I'll call Ryleigh. See you tomorrow in Pennsylvania. And… thanks."

"No need to thank me. This is Tex we're talking about."

The connection ended and Wolf quickly searched the Internet for contact info on The Refuge. He and Caroline had gone there to attend a wedding, but instead they'd found themselves in the middle of a revenge plot against the very woman he now hoped to talk to. He quickly dialed the number and waited impatiently for someone to answer.

"The Refuge. How may I help you?" a woman said when she answered the phone.

"My name is Matthew Steel. I need to talk to Ryleigh, please."

The woman hesitated a beat before she replied with exaggerated politeness, "May I ask the nature of your call?"

Wolf took a deep breath. He needed to calm the fuck down and not sound like a psycho here. "My wife, Caroline, and I were there not too long ago when Ryleigh was having some…difficulties."

"Oh! That's right! I remember you. This is Alaska. How are you?"

"Not good. Tex has disappeared. I need to talk to Ryleigh about helping me find him."

"What the hell? Tex is missing?"

Wolf supposed he was going to get that response from everyone he talked to, because it was so incomprehensible that the man who was instrumental in finding so many people in their circles had been kidnapped himself. He quickly summed up the situation for Alaska, internally itching to talk to Ryleigh.

But he understood, and approved of, Alaska being the gatekeeper for anyone cold calling The Refuge to talk to a staff member. Everyone who lived and worked there had been through their own traumas, and they couldn't be too careful.

"If you give me your number, I can run over to her cabin and see if she's around."

Wolf quickly rattled off his number.

"Give me three minutes. Four, tops. I know she's gonna want to call you back immediately," Alaska told him.

"I appreciate it." Wolf ended the connection and went into his bedroom to pack. Caroline wasn't home yet, but she should be on her way. She'd been visiting My Sister's Closet, her friend Julie's consignment shop in downtown Riverton. He didn't want to give her such upsetting news over the phone while she was driving.

He hadn't even gotten halfway through packing —and he was rushing—when his phone rang.

"Wolf," he said by way of greeting.

"Tell me you're shitting me," the woman on the other end said.

"Ryleigh?"

"Yeah. What the hell happened?"

For what seemed like the hundredth time, Wolf explained what he'd learned from Melody.

"What about Hope and Akilah? Are they all right? Are they in danger? Do you think whoever took Tex and Melody will go after them?"

Wolf's blood ran cold. The thought of either of Tex's girls having to go through the trauma that their parents had was unfathomable.

"Hope is covered. I'm not sure about Akilah."

"I'm on it," Ryleigh said, and Wolf heard keys clicking in the background. It was such a familiar sound, something he'd heard so often when he'd talked to Tex, that he immediately relaxed a fraction.

"Right. So, we need to find out who and why. That's the first step."

"Exactly. I've already talked to Beth. Elizabeth Turner. She's also working on this," Wolf told her.

"Good. She's amazing. No offense though, I'm better. Has there been a ransom or any communication from whoever took him?" she asked, her tone brusque.

"Melody said a brick painted bright yellow was on the road near her, after she was thrown out of the van. There was a note wrapped around it but she didn't touch it because she was afraid to contaminate any DNA or fingerprints."

"Smart. Okay, I'll hack into the police department databases and see if anyone has started a report yet. Forensics might still be working on it."

Wolf should've been concerned by how nonchalantly Ryleigh talked about hacking into a government entity's database, but at this point, he didn't care who the fuck she hacked as long as it resulted in intel he could use to find his friend.

"I don't suppose he was wearing one of the prototype trackers he's been working on, huh?" Ryleigh asked.

"Not that I know of. But it's possible."

Ryleigh grunted. "I'll find out. It would make tracking him down a hell of a lot easier if he was."

Wolf thought that was the understatement of the century.

"You going out there? To Pennsylvania?" she asked.

"Yes."

"I'm thinking you should call Baker."

Wolf had heard of Baker. He was a former SEAL living out in Hawaii. He'd never met the man, he was older than Wolf and his friends, but from what he understood, he had almost as many connections as Tex. Except his connections were a little...darker. Which might be extremely useful.

"Good idea," he said.

"I'm texting you his numbers now," Ryleigh said, even as Wolf's phone vibrated in his hand. Pulling it away from his ear, he saw a text from an unknown number. He assumed it was Ryleigh's.

"I'm not going to fly out to Pennsylvania. I've got everything I need here. My computers are secure here, as is the wi-fi. I'll be in touch."

Then she hung up. Wolf wasn't offended. He was actually relieved that she and Beth were already working on their ends to find out any information they could.

Wolf continued to pack as he clicked on the phone number Ryleigh had sent him.

"What?" a deep gruff voice said as the man answered. "Who is this?"

"My name is Matthew Steel, otherwise known as Wolf. Do you know Tex?" He wasn't beating around the bush.

"Yes, why?"

"He's been kidnapped."

"The fuck you say!" Baker exclaimed. "Where?"

"Off his street in Pennsylvania."

"What's being done about it?"

The man didn't even ask questions about what happened. He was all business.

Wolf explained about Beth and Ryleigh, and how he was heading across the country as soon as he could.

"I'll meet you there. We're going to need boots on the ground to get our man back," Baker said. "How's his wife?"

"Not great," Wolf admitted. "She's pretty banged up from being thrown from a moving vehicle."

"Motherfucker. You think she'd find it weird if my wife came with me? She doesn't know Jodelle, but my woman is really good with people who've been through trauma, since she's been through her own."

Wolf didn't hesitate. "No. If that's something she might want to do."

"Oh, Jodelle will want to come. I'm sure. It'll take me longer to get there than you, since I'm coming from Hawaii, but I'll get there as soon as it's physically possible."

Wolf nodded. He hadn't even thought past getting to Pennsylvania to Melody's side as soon as he could. But Baker was right. In the meantime, hopefully Ryleigh and Beth could find out where Tex was being held. If they did, he'd need some backup when he went to retrieve his old friend.

"Appreciate it."

"You called Rex?"

"Rex?" Wolf asked. It seemed as if everyone he talked to had someone else for him contact. Truthfully, it was getting old, but he'd talk to as many people as necessary if it meant putting together the best team to get Tex back.

"Yeah. He lives in Colorado. Runs the Mountain Mercenaries. He's got contacts in the sex trade industry. Not that I think Tex was taken for that, but those lowlifes always know people who know people. Rex might be able to work some kind of angle to see if there's been any chatter about a plot against Tex."

Wolf nodded as he went into the bathroom to grab his toiletries. "I've got about five minutes before my wife gets home and I have to tell her the bad news. You got his number?"

"I'll text it to you. Assuming the number you're calling from is a good one to send that text to."

"It is."

"Right. I've got my own list of contacts. I'll get a hold of them to see what they know. These are men and women who live on the fringes of society. I'll be calling in every marker I have. By the time I get to Pennsylvania, I'll hopefully have a lead."

Wolf was feeling better about their odds of

finding Tex with every phone call he made. "Hopefully," he echoed.

"See you on the East Coast," Baker said, then ended the call.

The text he promised came through a minute later, and once more, Wolf clicked on the number he'd received. He only had a few minutes now to talk to this Rex person before Caroline walked through the door.

"The Pit."

Wolf blinked. He had no idea what The Pit was, or if the man who answered was the guy he needed to talk to. "Is Rex there?"

"Who is this?"

Wolf took a deep breath and introduced himself. "My name is Wolf. I'm a former SEAL and a friend of Baker's. He said you might be able to help me."

"With what?"

Wolf still had no idea if he was talking to Rex or not, but he didn't have time for this shit. "My friend Tex was kidnapped. We don't know by who, or why, or what they want. But Baker said Rex might be able to use his connections to find any scrap of information about this fucked-up situation, because right now we have dick. All we have is his wife all banged the hell up from being thrown out of a moving vehicle, two kids who are probably scared out of their minds and wondering where their dad is, and my best friend fucking missing.

"Now, will you please put Rex on the phone, so I can finish this call and figure out how the hell to tell my own wife that one of *her* best friends has been brutalized, and the man who helped track her down when *she* was kidnapped is fucking missing?"

"This is Rex. I'm on it. Tex is the one man who I've never—and I mean *never*—heard one bad thing about. And trust me when I tell you that I've seen the worst humanity has to offer. Baker's also a good man. He's on this?"

"Yes. He's meeting me in Pennsylvania so if we do find Tex, he can go with me to get him back."

"Good. And you'll find him. There's no other alternative. I'll send out some feelers. See what people know. Anything else you need? More boots on the ground?"

Wolf sighed in relief. He'd take any help he could get. "Intel. That's what I need," he told this mysterious Rex.

"I'll see what I can do. This a good number to use to contact you if I find out anything?"

"Yes."

"Then I'll be in touch."

The phone went dead in Wolf's ear just as he heard Caroline pull into the driveway. He threw his toiletry bag into his duffel and zipped it before throwing it over his shoulder and heading out of the room to meet his wife. This wasn't going to be an easy conversation, and he was already dreading it.

CHAPTER 6

"Hi, hon," Caroline said as she walked into the house.

"We need to talk," Wolf said, not wanting to drag this out.

Her face fell and she put her purse down on the kitchen counter. Her gaze went to his duffel bag before it went back to his face. "You going somewhere?"

Wolf put his bag down and reached for Caroline's hand. He gripped it tightly and brought her over to the couch, where he pulled her down next to him.

"You're scaring me. What's wrong?" she asked.

"Tex is missing," Wolf said as gently as he could.

Caroline blinked. Then she smiled and rolled her

eyes. "Good one. Although that was in extremely poor taste as a joke. What do you want for dinner?"

"I'm being serious, Ice. Tex is missing. I got a call from Melody earlier. They were ambushed in their car on their street and shoved into a van. They both had hoods put over their heads as they were driven away. Then Melody was pushed out of the vehicle while it was moving, and the kidnappers disappeared with Tex."

His wife stared at him for a beat before her lips pressed together. Tears sprang into her eyes, but she blinked them back. "Is Melody okay?"

"Broken arm, concussion, road rash. But alive," Wolf said succinctly.

"And the girls?"

"Akilah is at college and will be picked up to be brought home. And Hope is with Amy and her husband."

"Tex?" Caroline whispered.

Wolf shook his head. "We don't know. We have no intel."

She sat up straighter. "None? Who took him? And why? Do they want money?"

"We don't know yet. But I've got people on this, honey."

"Who? What people? Tex can't be missing! He's

the one who finds everyone *else* who disappears!" Her voice had risen, and she sounded almost hysterical as she continued. "Was he wearing a tracker? He insists on everyone else wearing one, but I bet he wasn't, was he? It would help a whole hell of a lot if he practiced what he preached! Does he think he's invincible?!"

Wolf took Caroline's face in his hands and leaned closer. "I'm on this," he told her firmly.

He watched as the strongest woman he'd ever met, his wife, the love of his life, pulled herself together. She closed her eyes, took a deep breath, and grabbed hold of his wrists. When she opened her eyes again, he could see she had control over her emotions once more. "Of course you are," she said. "When does your plane leave?"

That's what he loved about Caroline. She was levelheaded. Good in stressful situations. Lord knew they'd met in the most stressful situation he could imagine. A plane full of drugged passengers that was taken over by terrorists. Then there was the cabin she'd been stashed, which had blown up, with Caroline rescuing him from the resulting fire —and *then* she'd been snatched while he'd been lying unconscious on the ground. And of course, the whole being-thrown-into-the-middle-of-the-ocean thing, while bound with weights around her ankles.

Yes, his Ice was a rock. And Melody needed her. Hell, *Wolf* needed her.

"In a couple of hours."

"I'm going with you," she informed him.

"Of course you are," Wolf said calmly.

Her eyes filled with tears once more. "He's really missing?"

"Yeah."

"Shit, Matthew."

"I know."

"He's the one we all call when people we know need help. Who do we call when the hunter becomes the hunted?"

"Everyone," Wolf said with conviction.

"And you've called everyone?"

"Not yet. But it seems like it. I've called the people who can help the most in the short term. Beth from Texas, Ryleigh from The Refuge, Baker from Hawaii, Rex from Colorado...we're all on this, sweetheart."

She sniffed, then nodded. "I need to pack." Caroline leaned forward and put her forehead against Wolf's. They sat like that for a beat before she abruptly stood. "Melody has to be freaking out. I can't believe they threw her out of a moving car! What *assholes*! Are the others coming too? Dude, Benny, the girls?"

"No, just us. The last thing Melody needs is a house full of people she'll have to worry about hosting," Wolf said.

"You're right. But what if Tex needs help? I know you're badass and all, but I'd feel better if you had some backup."

Lord, he loved this woman. "That guy I mentioned earlier...Baker? He's coming too."

Caroline lifted a brow. "One guy? That's it?"

"Believe it or not, I'm hoping none of us will even be necessary. But if it turns out we need help, you know I won't hesitate to call the guys. Tex will either escape himself or someone will find the intel we need to get the cops to go arrest those responsible."

"Or he could be—"

Wolf put his hand over Caroline's mouth, not letting her finish her sentence. "He's not. This is Tex. He's probably hurting, but he's *fine*."

Wolf hoped saying the words aloud would make them true.

Caroline pulled Wolf's hand away from her mouth. "Statistics say if someone isn't found within forty-eight hours, most of the time much less, it's likely they've been...you know."

"Women. I think that statistic mostly applies to women and kids. Those taken for sexual reasons. This is different." Wolf was talking out his ass. He had no intel as to why Tex was taken. But he was pretty sure it wasn't for sex. He wasn't a spring chicken anymore. None of them were. He couldn't personally fathom a situation where someone went to the lengths they had to kidnap a badass like John Keegan. But a man with the connections he had? With the intellectual prowess he had? There was a reason he was taken, and Wolf was pretty sure it wasn't just so he could be killed immediately.

Caroline stared at him for a long moment, then finally nodded. "I'm going to go pack."

"Okay, Ice. We'll head to the airport as soon as you're done."

"Can I call the girls? Or maybe just Fiona? She's going to take this the hardest. You know what Tex did for her when she had that flashback after she'd gotten home from being abducted herself."

Wolf couldn't deny his wife anything. "Just Fiona."

"I love you, Matthew."

"I love you too."

"Will you please think about wearing a tracker now?"

Wolf couldn't help but smile. Leave it to his wife to push her advantage. He'd been adamant about not wanting to be an experiment for Tex's newest tracker. Subcutaneous, tiny, undetectable to normal scanners.

"Go pack," he urged, knowing what his answer would be. If Tex was found, he'd happily be a guinea pig for his friend's newest innovation in trackers.

When Caroline was out of earshot, he pulled his phone out of his pocket once more. He needed to give Cookie a head's up that his wife was about to get some very bad news, and she'd need him by her side as soon as she was done talking to Caroline.

TEX SWALLOWED the groan that threatened to escape. His head was pounding. The damn music hadn't turned off for one second after he'd been put back into the box. He had no idea how much time had passed. He didn't think it had been too long though. Was it night? He wondered what Melody was doing. If she'd told Hope about him being taken. He prayed

Akilah was all right as well. He worried about her being away at school.

Pushing himself up, he got to his foot. He was hunched over since he couldn't stand up straight, and sweat poured from his temples as he struggled to overcome the pain in his body. He needed to stay mobile. Be ready for anything his kidnappers had planned. He couldn't just sit around being morose and depressed. No, he had to keep his body in tip-top shape. He hadn't had anything to eat since he'd been here, but he could live without food. Water was another story.

He'd already had to piss in a corner of the box, which hadn't made Tex happy in the least. He wondered if his kidnappers had thought about that part of keeping him confined or if they just didn't care if he had to live in his own waste. Probably the latter.

Tex racked his brain to try to think about who might be behind his kidnapping. He dealt with some horrible people, but no one lately who seemed any more horrible than others. They were all lowlifes. Kidnappers, sex traffickers, drug dealers...anyone and everyone who felt it was all right to use other people for their own gain.

Which made him think about what his own

kidnappers wanted. If they'd wanted him dead, they would've already killed him. That, at least, was a positive thing about this fucked-up situation. Intel? Money? Who knew. He supposed it didn't matter. Kidnapped was kidnapped.

Tex had a whole new sympathy for those he helped. Soldiers, women, children, friends...he'd worked hard on the back end to find out why and where and who. But he hadn't stopped to truly think about what the captives went through. He supposed it was because if he did, he wouldn't be able to do his job as effectively. But now he had nothing but time to think about those things.

Now, he felt as if he'd been insensitive. Or at least not sympathetic enough. He'd sat in his basement clicking away at his keyboard, giving the information he found to those who could go out and do the hard work of getting their friends or loved ones back.

He made a vow that if he got out of this alive, he'd do better. He'd recommend psychiatrists, places like The Refuge for victims to go to deal with what happened. Check in with their families more often. He wouldn't simply call it a job well done and slap his hands together as if all was back to normal.

Nothing for the people and families who went

through something like this was ever normal again. He should've known that better than anyone else.

Taking a deep breath and going to his happy place in his head...anywhere Melody was...Tex dropped to his knee and prepared to do some push-ups. He needed to stay busy. Strong. He had no idea how long he'd be here, so he'd do whatever he could to keep his body in working order. He was taking the fact that he wasn't already dead as a good sign. The assholes who took him wanted something. He just had to wait. Let his friends figure this shit out.

They'd do it too. Of that, he had no doubt. But there was a small niggling of concern about what his condition would be when they did.

CHAPTER 7

MELODY HADN'T SLEPT at all. Not even a catnap. The conversation with Hope was horrendous. Her daughter hadn't fully understood what she was hearing, and when she finally did? She'd fallen apart. John had always been larger than life to Hope. Her daddy. To hear that someone had hurt him and stolen him away? It was too much for her to bear.

Thank goodness Amy had been there to help console her. Melody had done her best, but she was grieving too. Was still in shock herself.

Amy had taken over. She'd made a noodle casserole for dinner, something neither Melody nor Hope ate much of. She'd done her best to answer all of Hope's questions and gotten her settled in bed. She'd held Melody's hand as she talked to Akilah, once more explaining everything that had happened that day. Melody had downplayed her injuries, not wanting to alarm her daughter. She was relieved when Akilah said she'd come home the next day.

Even though Amy had to be exhausted herself, she'd sat up with Melody until the wee hours of the morning. Though it was kind of a relief when Amy finally headed to the guest room, where her husband had gone to bed after doing several perimeter checks of the property.

But Melody hadn't gone to her own room, as she'd promised her best friend she'd do in "just a minute." Her arm was throbbing—hell, her entire body hurt—but that wasn't what was keeping her up. It was wondering what John was going through. Where he was. If he was okay.

She couldn't stop herself from reliving everything that had happened. Wishing she'd done things differently. Wondering if, had she been able to outrun the asshole chasing after her, today might've had another outcome. Maybe if the kidnappers hadn't been able to use her to make John comply, he would've been able to get away. Or she might've been able to get the attention of one of their neighbors, who could've called the cops.

She also couldn't stop wondering why this was

happening. What the people who'd attacked them and taken John could possibly want. Honestly, all the what-ifs were driving her crazy. She needed information. Needed to know why this happened.

Melody was standing in the kitchen, holding a cup of coffee and staring out the window sightlessly, when a knock at the door startled her so badly, she jerked and almost dropped her cup. She stared at the door for the longest time, afraid to move. What if the men had changed their minds about letting her go and had come back to get her?

No, that was stupid. They wouldn't knock on the freaking door. Taking a deep breath, she tried to slow her heartbeat. She put down the mug of coffee and debated what to do.

"Mel? It's me. Caroline. And Matthew."

Every muscle in Melody's body relaxed. She practically ran toward the front of the house. She heard Amy behind her, asking who was at the door, but Melody didn't stop. She barely remembered to turn off the alarm before unlocking the bolt to the front door and wrenching it open. As soon as she saw Caroline and Wolf, she burst into tears. She'd been holding herself together fairly well, but something about the sight of John's oldest friend had her completely breaking down.

Caroline stepped into the house and wrapped her arms around Melody, leading her back inside and toward the couch. It took several minutes of crying before Melody was able to get control of her emotions once more.

"Mel, did you get *any* sleep last night?" Amy asked.

She thought about lying, but these were her friends. Her rocks. She shook her head.

"Right. First up...a nap," Caroline announced, standing and pulling Melody up with her. As they headed down the hall toward her room, she balked.

"Not there. I...can't. Not without John."

She didn't need to say anything else. Caroline turned toward the room Akilah used when she was home instead. To Melody's surprise, her friend climbed onto the bed, pulling on her hand. Melody was too tired to resist. She let Caroline put her arms around her and sighed as she held her tightly.

"Matthew's here now. He's on this," Caroline said softly, running a hand over the top of Melody's head as if she were five instead of a grown woman. "He called all the people who have the skills to find him. There's a guy from Hawaii flying in today. Beth and Ryleigh are computer geeks like Tex...no offense. And they're *pissed*. Ryleigh isn't coming here, but I wouldn't be surprised if by the time we got up from our nap, they had this entire fucked-up situation solved. There's also a guy in Colorado talking with his contacts…and I guess there are a lot of them in some not-so-good circles.

"All I'm saying is…we've got this. Tex has had so many people's backs for so long, everyone is doing everything in their power to have his now. Sleep, Melody. It'll make you feel better."

"I want him home," she whispered.

"I know you do. And Matthew and the others do too. They're doing everything in their power to make that happen."

Amazingly, simply hearing that Wolf was on this, that there were people all over the country doing what they could to find her husband, allowed Melody to close her eyes and sleep. Finally.

Hours later, she woke up feeling surprisingly much better. Her heart still ached and her body still throbbed from all her injuries, but mentally, she felt stronger. Caroline wasn't in the bed with her anymore.

After visiting the bathroom, Melody made her way into the living room—and blinked at seeing all the people. Amy and her husband were still there, as were Wolf and Caroline. Hope and Akilah were sitting in a corner, talking quietly. But there were also three other people she'd never met before.

An older-looking gentleman with black hair liberally sprinkled with silver. He was good-looking, but he also had an air of danger surrounding him that made Melody nervous. He was standing next to a woman with dark brown shoulder-length hair. She reminded Melody a lot of Caroline. She had a look of kindness about her. It seemed crazy that she'd be able to tell that just by looking at someone, but Melody had a knack for sensing those things.

Then there was another man who out of place. He was leaning against the kitchen counter, simply observing everyone else. He seemed a little disconnected from the others but no less…capable? Melody didn't know what other word to use to describe him. He had the same vibe John and his badass friends had, but maybe a little muted. He had short brown hair and gray eyes that seemed to be taking everything at once. He was the first to notice Melody standing at the fringes of the room.

He cleared his throat and nodded in her direction.

"Melody! You're up!" Caroline said, as she hurried toward her.

"Mom!" Hope exclaimed, also running toward Melody.

She hugged her daughter and reached for Akilah, who'd followed her sister. The three Keegan women huddled together for a long moment.

"How're you two doing?" she asked quietly.

"We're hanging in there," Akilah said. "How're you? Your face looks horrible."

Melody chuckled. "Thanks."

Akilah blushed. "I didn't mean that the way it sounded."

"I know you didn't. And I'm okay. I promise."

"Mom, all these people are here to find Dad," Hope said.

"I know, honey."

"The guy with the silver hair says fuck a lot," Hope whispered.

Melody heard chuckles from around the room. Her daughter wasn't as discreet as she'd meant to be. "Well, he's an adult. He's allowed. You aren't."

"I know."

Looking up, Melody caught Matthew's gaze. He looked impatient, as if he had something important he wanted to tell her. With all these people here, she hoped someone had information about John. She looked at her daughters once more. "I'm going to need you guys to hang out in Hope's room for a bit. Can you do that for me?"

"I want to hear about Dad," Hope whined.

"I know you do, and I'll tell you what I can, when I can. Right now, I need you to do as I say. Please," Melody said.

For a second, she thought her strong-willed daughter was going to protest. But then she nodded and hugged Melody once more. "Okay, Mom."

"Thank you, baby."

"Come on, squirt. I want to hear all about school. This new boy you like, mean girls, and your friends," Akilah said.

Melody was grateful for such an understanding daughter. She had no doubt Akilah didn't care about any of those things, but the fact that she was willing to let the adults talk without Hope being able to overhear was a blessing.

The second the girls were out of earshot, Melody turned to Matthew. "What do we know?"

"Melody, I'd like to introduce you to some people. This is Baker Rawlins, and his wife Jodelle. They live in Hawaii and just got here thirty minutes ago. And this is Cade Turner. He lives in San Antonio with his wife Elizabeth. She's currently downstairs, working on hacking into Tex's computer. I'm not sure how much luck she'll have with it, but she said something about working with Ryleigh, who's still out in New Mexico. I'm sure those two will be able to find a way in."

Thinking of anyone at John's computers made Melody extremely uncomfortable, but she swallowed the feeling down. If it would help find her husband, she didn't care who did what. "It's nice to meet you," she said politely, nodding at the three newcomers to the house.

"Right, so Ryleigh called earlier. She discovered what the note said, tied to that brick you found said," Matthew said.

Melody froze. "She did? Did she talk to the detective?"

Baker snorted. "Fuck no. That fucker lips's are sealed tighter than a camel's ass in a sandstorm. She hacked into the files at the police station."

The first thought Melody had was that Hope was right. This man *did* say fuck a lot. But she wasn't offended. Not in the least. If ever there was a situation that warranted the prolific use of a swear word, it was this one. "What did it say?" she asked the room in general, afraid to know but needing answers all the same.

"They want money," Matthew said quietly.

For some reason, Melody was relieved beyond measure. If all it took was money, she'd have her husband back before anything horrible could happen to him. "Awesome. We can do that. How much?"

No one in the room would meet her gaze—which was Melody's first indication that something was really wrong. "Matthew?" she asked.

"A billion," Baker said.

For a second, the amount didn't register. When it did, Melody stumbled where she stood. Both Caroline and Amy rushed toward her. But Melody held out her hand, stopping them. "A *billion* dollars? Why in the hell do they think we have that kind of money? I mean, John has done well, but not *that* well. That's insane!" The last two words were practically shouted.

"It *is* insane," Baker agreed. "And it's bullshit. They don't want money. I mean, they do, but they also know that amount will be impossible to deliver."

Melody felt bile rise up in her throat. "So why? What *do* they want? And...why haven't the cops reached out to me and told me about the ransom?"

Once again, no one was meeting her gaze. She turned to look at Baker. A little rough around the edges, he was obviously the one least likely to beat around the bush. He'd tell her the way it was. "Baker?"

"Probably because the police think it's a joke. And we aren't sure what they really want yet. Just that the money seems to be a ruse. But just in case it isn't, we've put out the word for assistance in raising it."

Melody scoffed. "There's no way we can raise that much," she muttered.

"Actually, I think we can," Matthew said. "Word's spreading that Tex needs help. Money's been pouring in all morning. From *everywhere*. Anyone Tex has ever helped is doing what they can to return the favor. Last Beth told us, there was over two hundred million in the account she set up."

Melody stumbled to the couch and lowered herself onto the cushions. "Seriously?" she whispered. That kind of money was unfathomable to her.

"Everyone loves Tex," Caroline said from where she'd sat next to her. "And it's not just the people Tex has helped who are donating. Those people are contacting anyone and everyone *they* know. CEOs, men and women in the government, millionaires. It seems Tex has a reputation and everyone wants to make sure they help out, just in case they, or someone they love, need Tex's services in the future."

"So what now? If they don't really want money, how do we get John back?"

Before anyone could answer her, Cade's phone rang. Everyone turned to him expectantly. He answered it and put it on speaker.

"You're live," Cade said.

"Right, so I'm in," a woman on the other end said. "Of course, Tex being Tex, he doesn't have nicely organized files. They're encrypted and they're labeled all wonky. He's got folders that say 'recipes' that obviously aren't full of fucking recipes. It's gonna take Ryleigh and me a while to see if I can find anything; to research the hundreds or thousands of names of people he's helped and filter through the intel he's gathered in the process of finding the missing."

"Beth, Melody's up. She's here and knows about the note," Cade said gently.

"Beth is Elizabeth, from the basement," Amy said. "It's too hard for her to come up and down the stairs every time she finds something, so she just calls Cade when she needs to talk to us."

Melody sniffed slightly. "John does the same thing. Calls or texts me from the basement when he wants to tell me something. A lot of times it's just to tell me he loves me. With those calls, I always assumed he was working on a particularly nasty case, and it made him want to make sure I knew how much I meant to him." Even thinking about those calls made Melody tear up. But she blinked away the moisture. Now wasn't the time to cry.

"Hi, Melody. I'm so sorry this happened. But we're all on it. I hacked into the security system of your neighbor closest to where you and Tex were taken. Unfortunately, they've got motion-activated cameras, not the kind that are constantly recording. It caught the van coming straight at you guys, men dressed all in black with cloths covering their faces, getting out and going to Tex's side and hitting him. I saw you get out of the other side of the car and run out of frame, followed by one man, then another. It caught a scream—assuming that was you—and then the camera goes dark. It started up again thirty seconds later when a fucking bird flew in front of the camera, but the street was empty. I wasn't able to get a plate number because there *was* no plate. But we're working other angles."

Melody's hopes faded. She knew the importance of cameras. How they could practically solve cases for the cops…and for her husband as well.

"Traffic cameras?" she asked hopefully.

"Working on it. But without a plate, not sure

what good they'll do. We know where you were let out—"

Melody snorted.

"Sorry. Bad choice of words. Where you were pushed out of that fucking van, and we can get footage from convenience stores and banks along the route, but I'm not sure those will give us any useful intel. I think they'll just be a waste of time that we could use to do something else," Beth said.

It was a little weird to be talking to the woman through the phone when she was literally down the stairs from where they were, but Melody was getting a lot of information in a short period of time, and her head was spinning too much to care.

"So we don't have any information about who took him or where he is?" Melody asked.

"Not exactly," Baker said. "I spoke with Rex this morning. He's out in Colorado, and he's been talking to his contacts and researching all night. He's been able to verify that none of the major sex trafficking players are involved. We thought maybe they were, because Tex has interrupted a lot of their operations. Had a hand in freeing large groups of women and children who cost people a lot of money. But from what Rex has been able to find out, people in those circles know better than to fuck with Tex. They know what he's capable of, and while they hate losing money, they know they'll lose a hell of a lot more if they dared to attempt to take Tex out of the equation. Besides, honestly, they aren't smart enough to pull this off."

Melody was both relieved and horrified. "Okay, so then who?"

"We're working on it," Beth said. "On another note, Ryleigh said that Tex isn't wearing one of his newfangled trackers. Sorry."

"Darn," Melody said. She hadn't thought he was, but she'd held out a glimmer of hope that maybe he'd decided to test it on himself. That would've made this so much easier.

"I'm still working some of my angles," Baker said. "I know people in some pretty dark places. I pulled some markers, and they'll get back to me if and when they have something to report."

Melody was grateful for every single person in the room—and not in the room—for what they were doing to try to help. But she couldn't help but think, deep down, that John was in terrible trouble here.

"Any fingerprints or DNA on the brick and the note?" she asked, already knowing the answer.

"No. Nothing," Beth said.

"So what now?" Melody asked.

"We keep collecting money and turning over every rock. We're going to find him, Melody. I promise," Matthew said.

She looked down at her hands in her lap. It wasn't much of a plan, but she had to trust John's friends. They wanted him found as much as she did. She had to be patient, which sucked. Because thinking about what John might be going through while his friends did their thing made her sick to her stomach. Deep down, she knew he was suffering. Whoever took him had wanted him to hurt. Wanted him to be miserable. She knew that by the way they'd beaten him in their car. The way they so callously pushed her out of the van in front of him.

A knock on the door startled Melody, and she watched as Baker stalked over to it. He didn't bother to look through the peephole, simply wrenched it open. They all heard him ask, "Who are you?"

"Move," a young, feminine voice barked.

Glancing toward the foyer, Melody saw a woman in her early to mid-twenties enter the living room. She had shoulder-length dirty-blonde hair and blue eyes. She was wearing black boots, khaki cargo pants, and a long-sleeve black shirt. Her eyes were wild as she looked around the room, taking in everyone there.

"Annie Fletcher? What the hell are you doing here? Does your father know where you are?" Matthew asked.

The young woman glared at him. "Of course he does. As soon as he called, I asked for emergency leave and headed this way. What do we know and what can I do to help? And don't say nothing. I'm not eight years old anymore. I'm a fucking green beret. I might not be able to hack into a computer, but I can still help. Especially since people always discount me until they find my KA-BAR between their eyes."

Melody blinked. She knew Annie. Had heard stories about her from John often. He was extremely proud of the young woman she'd become. Had bragged about how fast she'd moved up the ranks, how she was a damn good soldier. Simply making it through the training to be a green beret wasn't an easy thing to do, but to do it as a woman was doubly impressive. John seemed to think she would continue to rise through the ranks and eventually be in charge of her own unit. For some reason, her being here made Melody feel a hell of a lot better. The power emanating from her was impressive.

"Damn glad to have you here," Baker said with a small nod.

"I can't wait to meet you!" Beth's voice shouted from the speaker of Cade's phone.

"So...what's happening?" Annie asked, all business.

Melody had no problem sitting back and letting the others take control of the conversation and the situation. She was out of her depth and she knew it. She'd been a closed-caption reporter...not a super soldier or computer genius. She was very grateful for every single man and woman working to find John, not to mention those who'd been so generously sending in money.

Her house was filled with the best of the best. They'd find her husband. The alternative was unthinkable.

CHAPTER 8

TEX HAD MOVED PAST WORRIED. Had embraced the pain he was feeling. Didn't give a shit about being naked as the day he was born. He'd moved into pissed-way-the-hell-off territory.

The assholes who'd taken him were giving him the minimal food and water necessary to keep him alive and that was about it. They'd finally thrown a bucket into his box—a day late and a dollar short—for him to use to relieve himself, but they still hadn't told him a damn thing. He thought it had been a few days since his abduction. All he could think about was Melody. How scared she must be. How worried. He wondered if she'd gotten a hold of any of his friends by now. What the police were doing to find him.

He had no doubt that a search was underway, and for the first time, *he* was the subject of that search. He was used to being on the other side. Figuring out clues and scouring electronic devices for any kind of intel. He was actually bored as fuck. And he had a headache from hell from the music his captors were still blasting. He'd figured it was to keep him from overhearing anything about where he was or what was said by anyone outside his little seven-by-three-by-five slice of hell.

As soon as he had the thought, the door to his box opened, sending painful rays of lights into his eyes once more. As in the past, the only thing he could do was shut his eyes to try to preserve his sight, and his captors took the opportunity to grab him.

They weren't gentle about it either, which wasn't a surprise. He stumbled on his foot as he was dragged out of the box and shoved into the uncomfortable wooden chair once more, binding him securely. Tex was pretty sure he was gonna get a splinter of these times from them handling him so violently. The thought almost made him grin. It would be hilarious when he was rescued if, out of this entire fucked-up situation, his only injury besides the results of the beatings was a fucking splinter in his ass.

But any kind of humor fled when his eyes adjusted to the light and he saw there were more people in the room than there'd ever been in the past. He could see his box set against one wall. Someone had built it specifically for keeping a person. He didn't know if he was the first "guest" these men had ever hosted, or if they did this all the time.

There was a window but it was covered by dark curtains. Tex could see a little bit of light coming through the bottom of the material, letting him know it was daytime. He wished he could see outside, even for a moment. Was he in a neighborhood? A farmhouse? A warehouse? He had no way of telling.

Looking at his captors, he saw they were wearing all black, same as the day he'd been taken. They had gloves on and masks covering their faces. It was difficult to tell what nationality they were. He could see they were all Caucasian though. It was a start. Tex filed the information away.

One of the men, who seemed to be in charge, nodded at another. The latter walked over to a stool sitting in the otherwise empty room...empty other than the fucking box, the chair he was sitting in, and of course, the four other men in the room.

"It seems as if your wife isn't cooperating," the man said.

Tex didn't recognize the man's voice. He had no discernable accent that he could detect. He needed intel, and the only way to get it was to antagonize this man. Get him to admit why he'd taken Tex in the first place. That was the only way to try to figure out who these men were and what connection they had to him. There had to be one. It was highly unlikely they'd randomly picked his car out of all the vehicles in the world to attack.

"Maybe if she knew who you were and why you took me, she'd be more willing to play your game," Tex said.

"How do you know I haven't already told her those things?" the man asked.

Tex smirked. "Because if you had, you'd be dead and I'd be home with my family."

That didn't go over well with the man. His brows furrowed, and Tex figured if he could see his mouth, he'd be frowning.

"So damn cocky," the man said with a small shake of his head. "You've always been the cockiest son-of-a-bitch out there."

So he *did* know Tex. He *knew* this was personal in some way. "Have we had the pleasure of meeting?" he pushed. He didn't think the man would answer, but maybe he was wrong. Some men took pleasure in bragging about themselves and what they'd done. With luck, this man would be one of them. There wasn't a lot Tex could do with the information, not naked and stuffed in a box, but when he was rescued, he could certainly make sure his captor and all his cronies couldn't fuck with anyone ever again.

"As I said, your wife isn't cooperating," the man repeated.

Tex frowned. The lack of intel was getting to him. He was a man of action. He thrived on ferreting out the tiniest bit of information about his target. His fingers itched for a keyboard and computer. He could find out who this asshole was. All he needed was the tiniest thread to pull.

"She obviously doesn't love you as much as you'd thought, does she?" the man asked, his voice louder.

Tex ignored him. Baiting him with Melody's love, or lack of it, wasn't going to work. Tex was very secure in his relationship with his wife. He'd do anything for her, would even die if it meant she would live. Which was a last resort, of course. He wanted to live. He had many more years of wedded bliss to experience.

"Are you listening to me?" the man yelled, losing some of the control he'd held onto since dragging Tex from the box.

"Yes," he said simply.

"We left a note saying we'd give you back if she paid a ransom. And so far, she doesn't seem interested in paying anything for your return."

"Did you tell her how to get in touch with you? Left a number? An email? Something?" Tex asked, his voice even and calm. "Because without that, she can't tell you that she's working on it, can she?" He didn't know how he knew exactly what to say to needle this man, but he did.

And he was right. His captors didn't want money. They would've called her or otherwise gotten in touch if they did. Given Melody a way to get the ransom to them.

Tex saw the other men in the room share looks of confusion. Now it was more than obvious that they weren't privy to the details of this kidnapping. They'd been brought in as muscle. For the intimidation factor...and they were obviously surprised that the request for money hadn't included any way for Melody to communicate with the man in charge.

"She doesn't fucking love you!" the man yelled, finally losing his temper. "The only reason she's with a *cripple* like you is because of your money. It's no wonder she doesn't want to pay. She wants to keep all that cash to herself. She's probably relieved she doesn't have to look at your disgusting stump anymore!"

Tex stayed calm. Nothing this man said hit its mark. Melody had no problem whatsoever with his disability, and she certainly didn't mind his scars or his "stump," as this asshole called his leg.

When the man saw he wasn't getting a rise out of Tex, he huffed out an agitated breath, then reached behind him.

That made Tex tense up for the first time. He knew what that movement meant—and he was right. His captor pulled a pistol from a holster at the small of his back and pointed the weapon at Tex.

"How do you think she's gonna feel when she hears you being shot on tape?" the man asked, stepping closer to Tex.

Looking into the barrel of the gun made Tex break out in a sweat for the first time. He didn't want to die. But he wasn't going to give in to this man. Hell, the man hadn't even really pumped him for any kind of information. Wasn't threatening him to get him to talk. Tex wasn't sure why the man was so pissed off. But he realized at that moment that this entire conversation was being recorded. That's what the man near the stool had done. Pressed record on a fucking tape player. Something from the eighties. Which was kind of smart considering Tex—and some of the men and women he worked with—would be able to trace an audio file sent via email.

"Don't comply!" Tex shouted, knowing the man planned on sending the tape to his wife to torture her. He was also pretty sure this wasn't about to be the end of his life. No, this asshole wasn't done with him. He was just getting started.

"Shut up!" the man ordered.

But Tex didn't shut up. "I love you, Mel. I'm fine! Don't give this asshole any money! Tell—"

He didn't get to finish his message of love for his children before a loud gunshot rang out through the room.

It took Tex a fraction of a second to realize that he wasn't shot in the head, or heart, or gut, any of which would've probably been fatal.

No, the asshole had shot him in the leg. The calf.

He let out an anguished, belated yell. The pain was immense. Almost overwhelming. "You asshole! What the fuck?!" he exclaimed.

"Maybe that will give your precious wife motivation to get the fucking money we asked for," the man said.

Through a red-hot haze of pain, Tex saw the man nod at the guy near the tape recorder. He clicked a button, then picked up the small device and left the room.

As the door opened, Tex saw what looked like some sort of living room, although not lived in for quite a while. But he didn't get a chance to see much more before the door shut behind the man who'd left.

"Put him back in the box. Let him think about things for a while," the man in charge ordered.

"Think about what?" Tex raged, struggling against the men who untied his hands and cut off the zip-tie they'd used to secure his now bleeding leg to the chair. "You haven't asked me a damn thing. You haven't requested I do anything. There's nothing to think about except how much of a coward you are! You won't even tell me what I've supposedly done to make you kidnap me in the first place!"

"You can think about how your precious Melody will feel when she gets that tape. When she hears you being shot and yelling in pain," the man said with no feeling whatsoever. Then he turned his back on Tex as he was being dragged back to the box.

Tex struggled, but it was no use. He was literally thrown back into the box, landing with a thud on the hard floor before once more being shut into the dark. A split second later, the loud music started again.

Tex threw back his head and screamed out his frustration and pain.

His captor wasn't wrong about his thoughts. It was all he *could* think about—Melody's reaction to hearing that gunshot and wondering what the hell was happening to him. Worrying that he'd been killed, and she'd had to listen to it. He just hoped she'd be able to think rationally enough to understand that him yelling *after* the shot went off meant he obviously wasn't dead.

Of course, he could still bleed out. Clasping his hands as tightly to his holes in his calf as he could to try to stop the bleeding, Tex rocked back and forth and clenched his teeth together as pain coursed through him.

He was essentially completely helpless now. With only one leg to stand on, literally, and that leg being shot, the only way he was getting out of this box was if he crawled...which he wasn't opposed to doing if it meant escaping.

Except there was no way out of this box. He'd thoroughly examined every inch of it with his hands in the last couple of days. The only way he was getting out was if someone opened the door and freed him. Damn it.

Frustration ate at him. His captors had the upper hand, of that there was no doubt. He needed his friends to hurry the hell up and figure this out. It was obvious the man in charge knew Tex. And he seemed especially fixated on Melody, which was terrifying. He could be trying to use his wife to torture Tex, or he could be planning something more nefarious. The thought of Melody being in the same situation he was right now was perhaps the only thing that could break Tex.

He prayed someone had gotten a hold of Ryleigh. The young woman was a fucking genius with computers and hacking. With her looking into his files—he had no doubt she could hack into his computer with no problem—she should be able to find something. Anything.

His other friends weren't exactly slouches either. Elizabeth, Baker, Wolf, Trigger, Mustang, Cookie, Cruz...if they all worked together they could figure this out. He just prayed they'd be able to do so before the lunatic with one hell of a grudge against him got a little too trigger happy and decided to cut his losses.

There was no way he would simply let Tex go at this point. No, it was either his friends figured this shit out, or Melody would be burying her husband.

It was that thought, along with the pain, that made Tex throw up. Not that there was much in his belly. Bile and a bit of water. He couldn't stand the thought of Melody's pain when she heard that tape.

"Come on, guys...I need you to figure this out and get me the hell out of here," he mumbled, unable to hear his own words over the volume of the heavy metal.

For a split second, he thought about Raiden and Khloe. How they'd been shoved into a trunk with death metal—the disgusting kind—blaring all around them. He hadn't understood the psychological and physical effects that sort of thing could have on a person until right this moment. He vowed if he lived through this, he'd call them and apologize for not finding them faster.

Doing his best to block out the music, Tex concentrated on his leg. He probed his aching calf and realized the bullet had gone straight through the fleshy part, which was a good thing. It meant he didn't have a bullet lodged inside him.

The asshole was a very good shot, which didn't make Tex feel all warm and fuzzy. He totally could've shot him somewhere that would've been fatal, and yet he hadn't. He'd chosen to give him a flesh wound, a very painful flesh wound, through his calf instead. Tex would've preferred to be dealing with an amateur. But with every minute that passed, he was learning that was anything but the case. This guy was good. But Tex was positive his team was better. They had to be if he was going to get out of this alive.

CHAPTER 9

THREE DAYS.

When all this started, if someone had told Melody this much time was going to pass without any word about where her husband could be, she would've lost it. But the days were all blurred together. She was barely sleeping, had to force herself to eat. Amy had taken Hope and Akilah back to her house to get them away from the constant stress and worry that had taken over the Keegan household. Cade had gone with them to help keep watch, make sure they were safe, and Rex, the guy from Colorado, had sent two additional men to help guard the girls. Melody thought they were introduced to her as Meat and Arrow, but she wasn't one hundred percent sure. She was just relieved someone was watching over her kids.

She paced back and forth, something she'd been doing almost nonstop. She'd probably walked twenty thousand steps today already. But she couldn't stay still. Couldn't stop wondering what in the world was happening. Where John might be.

In the meantime, people around the world had donated almost seven hundred million dollars. Including a very large donation from Steve Ballmer, who had connections to Microsoft, and even the richest billionaire in the world, Bernard Arnault, chairman and CEO of LVMH empire of seventy-five fashion and cosmetic brands transferred a large chunk of change because he'd once consulted with Tex about how to keep his five adult children safe from money grubbing kidnappers.

It boggled her mind. That kind of money was incomprehensible. Yet it wasn't enough. And it also didn't matter, because they'd received no instructions from John's kidnappers. Where to drop off the money. Proof of life. Nothing.

Beth hadn't slept much either; she'd been in John's office in the basement almost twenty-four-seven. She was constantly talking with Ryleigh, the woman in New Mexico. Together they were going through all of John's files, trying to figure out who was behind this kidnapping and why.

But it was all happening too slow for Melody's peace of mind. She wanted John back. Today. Now.

When Melody's cell phone rang—the phone she'd gotten back from the police—she jerked her head toward the sound. She lunged toward the counter, hoping against hope it was John calling to tell her he'd escaped and to come pick him up. It was a ridiculous thought, but she couldn't help hoping anyway.

But Wolf was standing right by the counter and reached the phone first. Melody watched him with wide eyes for any sign that whoever was calling had good news.

"Melody Keegan's phone...yeah, she's here, but you can talk to me... Wait—where? Seriously? Fuck. All right, someone will be there to get it. And we're gonna want to see the security tapes too... Are you fucking kidding me? Shit, fucking hell. *Fine.* You'll know who's there to pick it up, because he'll be the scary-as-fuck guy you don't want to mess with."

Then Wolf aggressively punched the off button on the phone.

"That was much more satisfying when phones could be slammed down," he muttered, before taking a deep breath and looking around at the people in the room.

Caroline and Jodelle had gotten close in the last few days. Jodelle was the sweetest woman, and in any other situation, Melody would've loved to have gotten to know her better. But all she could think about was John and what he might be going through.

Baker was never far from his wife's side, constantly checking in with her, making sure she ate, got enough water, and was doing all right during this very stressful situation. It reminded Melody of how John was with her, and it was equally painful and heartwarming at the same time.

Annie was still there, as well. She was like a cork ready to burst. She'd probably taken as many steps as Melody had. She wanted to be doing something, but because her skills didn't lie with computers, she had to wait until they had information to act on.

"That was an employee of the Stop-N-Go on Fourth and Main. He said a kid, a teenager, came into the store with a tape and Melody's phone number. Said he was told to go there and hand it over, and have someone call the number and tell the woman to come pick it up." Wolf held up his hand.

"But they have no security cameras. Oh, and the boy claimed the guy who gave him the tape said the clerk would pay him a hundred bucks to deliver it."

"You think he'll still be there when I get there?" Baker asked, obviously having no doubt he'd be the one going to get it.

Wolf snorted. "No. Because the clerk said the kid ran off when he refused to give him any money"

"I'm going too," Annie said.

"I'll tell Beth about the call," Jodelle said. She went over to Baker, went up on her tiptoes and kissed him, before heading for the basement door.

"Even without cameras at the Stop-N-Go, she can look at other cameras in the area to see if she can figure out what direction the boy came from. That might give us an idea of where he met up with whoever gave him the tape," Wolf muttered.

"Who the hell has something to play a *tape* on?" Caroline asked no one in particular. "I mean, is it an eight-track, a cassette tape, one of those smaller tapes used in recorders that were so popular with reporters back in the day? Or is it an actual electronic recording?"

"I think Hope has a cassette player," Melody said, her mind spinning. "We got it for her because she was obsessed with all things eighties when her elementary school had an eighties day. We found it at Goodwill, and they even had some tapes too. Debbie Gibson, Cyndi Lauper, Boy George..." She chuckled, but it wasn't exactly a humorous sound. "I never would've thought I'd need it to play a tape sent by my husband's kidnappers."

Caroline immediately went to Melody and put her arm around her waist in support.

"We'll be back as soon as we can. I'll call Beth if we get any intel while we're there," Baker said in a flat, no-nonsense tone. Then he and Annie were gone.

Melody trembled. She dreaded hearing what was on that tape, but at the same time, Baker and Annie couldn't get back fast enough. She needed to know what was happening with John. If he was all right. There was no guarantee he would even be on the tape, but she longed to hear his voice. To know he was still alive.

It felt like it took an eternity for Baker and Annie to return. Time seemed to stop as everyone waited. When Melody heard a car in the driveway, it was all she could do not to run out there and snatch the tape out of their hands.

Caroline had retrieved the tape player from Hope's room, and it was sitting on the counter when

Baker and Annie walked into the house, neither of them looking happy.

"The clerk had no info other than the boy was around thirteen, white, wearing jeans and a black T-shirt, and he'd never seen him before," Baker announced.

"Damn," Matthew muttered.

Melody almost didn't care about any of that. Her gaze was fixed on the tape in Annie's hand. The young woman saw the tape player on the counter and did a double take. "Where the hell did you get that? I told Baker we'd have nothing to play this thing on, but he wanted to get back as soon as he could because he knew Melody would be worried. Figured we could deal with finding something to play it on after we returned."

Melody shot the taciturn man a grateful smile. He was gruff and rough around the edges, but she liked him a lot. He also didn't try to hide anything from her. She appreciated that more than she could say. "I bought it for Hope last year when she was going through her eighties phase," she explained succinctly.

Annie nodded and walked over to the counter. She carefully inserted the tape, then looked up at Baker as if to ask if it was all right to hit play.

Melody wanted to growl. The only person she should be asking permission from to play the damn thing was *her*, but she held back her irritation. Everyone was only trying to help.

"Why don't you let us listen to this first," Matthew suggested gently.

Melody shook her head firmly. "No. Come on, Annie. Hit play," she demanded.

"Are you sure?" Baker asked. "We have no idea what's on there."

"John is my husband. I am *not* stupid. I'm perfectly aware that he might not be on this tape at all. That he could be dead. And you might think I'm hysterical, or simply wishing for things that aren't true, but I don't feel as if he's gone. Here. In my heart," Melody said, putting a hand on her chest. "I need to know what the next steps are. If they really did this for cash, I want to be able to give the money people have generously sent in to these assholes and get my husband back. I need him. Hope and Akilah need him. Hell, the *world* needs him. Sometimes it annoys me how often he's holed up in his basement, helping others, but I wouldn't want him to be any other way. Now play the damn tape, Annie!"

"Do it," Baker agreed, nodding at the young woman.

It felt as if everyone in the room was holding their breath as Annie finally pushed the play button on the tape recorder.

It seems as if your wife isn't cooperating, a man's voice said.

Melody shivered as the menace and hatred came through loud and clear through the scratchy tape.

Maybe if she knew who you were and why you took me, she'd be more willing to play your game.

Melody couldn't help but grin just slightly at her husband's words. He was right. She was more than willing to pay the asshole who'd taken John, but she needed to know *how* to do that.

How do you know I haven't already told her those things?

Because if you had, you'd be dead and I'd be home with my family.

So damn cocky. You've always been the cockiest son-of-a-bitch out there. As I said, your wife isn't cooperating. She obviously doesn't love you as much as you'd thought, does she?

Melody wanted to snort. John knew how much she loved him, because she told him every day. At least once. He was her everything, and he knew it.

Are you listening to me?

Yes.

Hearing John sounding so calm in the face of this asshole getting more and more worked up was satisfying. He'd always been that way. He had to be in order to do what he did. He had to stay calm when the shit was hitting the fan. John had once told Melody that staying calm was the best thing that anyone could do in a situation that was out of their control.

Melody realized she'd missed some of what was said because she was lost in her head, thinking about her husband, but the angry man's next words snapped her back to attention.

She doesn't fucking love you! The only reason she's with a cripple like you is because of your money. It's no wonder she doesn't want to pay. She wants to keep all that cash to herself. She's probably relieved she doesn't have to look at your disgusting stump anymore!

That pissed Melody off. She loved John for the man he was. She couldn't care less about what his leg looked like.

How do you think she's gonna feel when she hears you being shot on tape?

Her heart literally stopped beating in her chest. Melody gripped the edge of the counter and leaned forward, toward the tape player. She wanted to beg Annie to shut it off. She'd been so sure John was alive. That he was fine. She couldn't bear to hear him being shot on tape.

Don't comply!

For the first time, John's voice held a note of anxiety.

Shut up!

I love you, Mel. I'm fine! Don't give this asshole any money! Tell—

Melody gasped as the sound of the shot echoed through the kitchen. Her legs went weak and she collapsed to the floor, shock making it hard to think straight.

You asshole! What the fuck?!

Maybe that will give your precious wife motivation to get the fucking money we asked for!

There was a click—and the recording ended.

John! That was John swearing. He was alive...or had been right after that gunshot had gone off. Melody sat on the floor, shaking uncontrollably.

Caroline was immediately at her side, an arm around her shoulders, holding onto her.

To Melody's surprise, Baker knelt down next to her on the floor. He didn't touch her, just hovered in her personal space. "He's okay," he said firmly, in a low, deadly tone.

"You don't know that," Melody whispered.

"You heard him. He was pissed. If he'd been shot in the head, he wouldn't have been able to say a word. And if he was shot in the heart or gut, he most likely wouldn't be swearing at his kidnapper; he'd be swearing in general. Probably using his last moments to tell you how much he loves you."

Melody shivered at the picture Baker's words put in her head. But...he had a good point. "Do you think he was shot at and not actually hit?" she asked, hoping against hope Baker would say yes.

Instead, the man pressed his lips together.

Shit.

"Tex is smart. And tough as hell. He'll get through this. Just as you will. You're both relying on the other to stay strong. To have a clear head. To do what needs to be done," Baker told her.

Melody nodded, even though she felt anything but strong right now. "Did you get anything from that?"

"Get anything?"

"Yeah. Like clues or something?"

To her disappointment, Baker shook his head slightly. "Not really. But the clerk at the gas station told us the kid who dropped off the tape had a message. He said the money should be taken to the old Sugar Shack Mill tomorrow at eleven p.m.

sharp. No cops, no FBI, no one but you with the money."

Melody was shocked. "The Sugar Shack Mill? That's in the middle of nowhere. And it's long since been abandoned."

Baker nodded. "Annie did a quick search while we were on our way back here with the tape, and that's what she gathered from the Google Earth view, and from other intel she found online."

"Wait, does he want cash? Even I know that's impossible. First, there's no way we can get that much money. There simply isn't enough cash in the state. Second, all those bills would weigh a ton. Literally. Okay, I don't know exactly how much it would weigh, but that's ridiculous. Why wouldn't whoever has John request that it be transferred electronically?"

Melody felt much better talking about this kind of thing. She had no doubt she'd replay that horrible tape over and over in her head for the rest of her life, but for now, she was more than willing to think about anything other than her husband being shot.

"Because the asshole knows we can track any kind of money transfer."

Looking up, Melody saw Beth had come up out of the basement and was listening to her conversation with Baker. Everyone was. Jodelle, Matthew, Annie, Caroline…and apparently even Ryleigh from The Refuge in New Mexico. Beth was holding a phone, and the comment had come from the small speaker.

"But they've already messed up," Ryleigh continued from the other side of the country. "I've been studying the tape, separating out the voices from the background noises, putting the kidnapper asshole's voice through an analyzer, and I have a program that's searching through known samples of scumbags from all over the world to see if he matches up."

"And?" Matthew asked impatiently.

"Nothing yet, as I just started, but right before you guys got back with that tape, I'd narrowed down the list of people who might hate Tex so much they'd want to see him suffer. And those who have the smarts and connections to do something as ballsy as kidnapping him in the middle of the day, on a very public street."

"Woman," Baker threatened as he stood, taking Melody's upper arm in his hand and gently helping her to her feet as well. The difference in how he held Melody and the irritation in his voice was stark.

"Three people: Damien Nightshade, Vincent Coldridge, or Asher Rook."

"Wait, I know Nightshade," Matthew said, sounding shocked. "He was a sergeant when I was on the teams. We did an op with him. I can't remember where."

"Afghanistan," Ryleigh said. "And good memory. Yes, he was a medic, and before he worked with you and your team, he worked with Tex. His team was tasked with having Tex and *his* team's six as they infiltrated a stronghold of bad guys while trying to take out an HVT."

"That's a high-value target," Caroline whispered to Melody.

"I know," she said.

"He's done everything in his power to get the medals stripped that Tex and the rest of his team earned on that mission, because he claims *his* team was the one that rescued the group of civilians who got caught in the crossfire between the SEALs and ISIS."

"So he's holding a grudge," Matthew commented.

"Oh yeah. A big fucking grudge," Ryleigh agreed.

"And I know Coldridge," Baker said. "Or I know *of* him, at least. He's got connections with the Italian mafia in New York."

Melody wanted to ask how the hell Baker knew someone in the Mafia, but decided she was better off not knowing. "Why would he have a thing against my husband?" she asked instead.

"I don't know. But you can bet I'm going to find out," Baker said grimly.

"Because Tex tracking down a missing teenager exposed a multimillion-dollar gun-running operation run by Coldridge's family," Ryleigh said, as easily as if she was informing them all of the weather for the upcoming week. "He obviously didn't mean to, but the girl had run away with her boyfriend, who was part of the security team for a shipment of guns, and when the cops went looking for the girl, they found themselves drowning in weapons instead. Coldridge has never forgiven Tex for that, even though he didn't really have anything to do with exposing the gun-running operation. His missing girl was just in the wrong place at the wrong time."

"Fuck," Baker said.

Melody agreed with that sentiment a hundred percent.

"And the last guy? Asher Rook? Who's he?" Annie asked.

"Nobody," Beth answered, before Ryleigh could.

"Literally no one. He hasn't been in the military, doesn't have a ton of money or influence. Hell...he actually lives in his mom's basement. He's forty-three, not currently married, no kids, and only works sporadically. His favorite pastime is playing video games online."

"Why in the hell would he be on your list?" Baker asked. "From everything Melody said, the guys who took her and Tex seemed like professionals, and they know enough not to use any electronic means to communicate so they can't be traced."

"Well, five years ago, his wife disappeared. Just poof—gone. She went to a football game in Pittsburgh and never came home. The police never found any trace of her. Asher was interrogated, but there's been no evidence that he had anything to do with her going missing. Apparently, Rook had heard of Tex and contacted him, asking for help. But at the time, he was neck deep in a case, trying to find someone else. He told Rook he was sorry, but he couldn't help."

"Did they ever find her?" Melody asked quietly.

"No," Ryleigh said. "Nothing. No body, no clues whatsoever. Then, about a year ago, there was a flurry of activity on the dark web from Rook's mom's IP Address pertaining to Tex. Research..."

inquiries about everything from his life before he was in the Navy, to the missions he participated in while he was a SEAL, his medical records, and any and all mentions of Tex in the news."

"That doesn't mean Rook is involved. Especially if he doesn't have any military experience. Like Baker said, from what we saw on those surveillance cameras, the people who took Tex and Melody had skills," Matthew argued.

"Asher Rook has an IQ of 150," Ryleigh said.

"Holy crap, that's like...really smart," Melody said.

"Exactly. The average IQ is a hundred, genius is between 120 and 140...and that's only about two percent of the population."

"Then what's this guy doing living at home and mooching off his mom?" Annie asked. "He could be working for one of the top companies in the world. Making a ton of money."

"No clue," Ryleigh said. "But keep in mind that he's also spent hours upon hours playing video games. And his favorites are those military shoot-'em-up ones."

"Fuck."

"Shit."

"Damn."

Melody agreed wholeheartedly with her friends' assessment of the situation.

"All those hours were kind of research for him then," Baker said. "So are we thinking it's Rook?"

"I didn't say that," Ryleigh said patiently.

"But you didn't *not* say it either," Matthew argued.

"Look. It could be any of those three guys. Or someone I haven't found yet," Ryleigh told them.

"But you don't think so," Matthew said.

"I don't think so," Ryleigh confirmed. "I checked and Nightshade and Coldridge have rock solid alibis. That doesn't mean they couldn't have hired someone, or a whole slew of someones, to snatch Tex, but there's nothing about those two that is out of the ordinary for them. No phone calls to unknown numbers. No money being transferred out of any of their offshore accounts. They're just going along with their miserable lives at the moment."

"So what are our next steps? Melody was right, how the hell does he expect her to bring that much cash to the drop point?" Baker asked.

"It's not about the money. It never has been for him," Matthew said grimly. "It's about winning the game. About revenge. He didn't help Asher find his wife, so he wants Tex to suffer."

"He's never going to let John go, is he?" Melody whispered.

The look of compassion and regret on Matthew's face almost made Melody's legs buckle again.

"I doubt it, no," he said after a long moment.

"So what's the point of all this?" Melody yelled, fed up with everything. She'd reached her breaking point. It hadn't been that long, but every day that passed seemed like an eternity. A part of her, a very *small* part, was empathetic toward this Asher guy. It had to have been horrible to not know where his wife was or what had happened to her. He'd gotten no closure whatsoever. But to take out his frustration and anger on her and her family because John had been busy saving someone else? That was unacceptable.

"Why have me bring money to that abandoned factory in the middle of the fucking night if he isn't going to let John go?"

"Because he wants *you* to suffer, as well," Ryleigh said calmly.

Melody didn't want to hear that. Didn't like how the other woman seemed so unaffected by this entire situation.

Reaching out, she grabbed the coffee cup she'd used earlier and threw it as hard as she could against the living room wall. It shattered into a thousand pieces.

"And I want *you* to care!" she shouted at the phone, wishing the woman she was aiming her ire at was standing in front of her. "I want you to sound as if you give a shit, not like you're reciting what you need to buy at the damn grocery store later! And I want my husband back!"

No one said a word.

All Melody could hear was her own harsh breathing. Caroline's hand landed on her shoulder, but she shrugged it off. Her gaze was locked on the phone in Beth's hand, willing the apparently amazing Ryleigh—who John thought was better than him at hacking—to say something that would make her feel better.

Instead, her words made Melody feel worse.

"I care. Tex made me feel…worthwhile for the first time in my life. As if I wasn't a freak for knowing how to do the things I can do with a computer. He told me he admired me. That if his daughters turned out half as smart, kind, and resourceful as I am, that he'd consider it a blessing. And the fact that someone dared use *you* to get to him pisses me off, because I was once used as bait and leverage, just as you were. But if I take the time to think about it too much, I won't be able to do my job. If it makes you feel better, after this is over and Tex is back home, I'll completely fall apart and probably have to spend several sessions with our in-house psychiatrist, Henley, here at The Refuge."

"I'm sorry. Shit, I'm so sorry. I'm being a bitch," Melody said, her voice hitching. "You probably haven't slept much in the last three days either, and I'm here being ungrateful and horrible. I know you care. Everyone does. Because that's the kind of man *John* is. He cares about everyone, wants to protect the world from evil, so I know the people he's closest to would feel the same. I just...I'm so worried. And frustrated about what to do next."

"Ryleigh, where is Asher now?"

Everyone turned to stare at Annie. She was standing away from the others a bit, her hands in fists, and she...looked...*pissed.*

"At this exact moment, I'm not sure. As I said earlier, he lives with his mom in a neighborhood north of the town of Washington. Why? What are you thinking?"

"People with high IQs are book smart, but sometimes they aren't the best at dealing with real-world stuff. What if he's got Tex nearby?"

"Nearby how?" Baker barked.

"I don't mean in his mom's house, that would be too obvious, even for him. But are there any abandoned houses in the neighborhood or within a reasonable distance? Or...I'm assuming he wouldn't have him stashed at the money-drop factory, but is there somewhere in between that and his home that could be a possibility?"

They all heard fingers typing on a keyboard. "I don't know. I need to look," Ryleigh said.

"We've got until tomorrow at eleven at night to figure things out," Annie said.

"No way in hell is Melody going to that drop," Matthew said firmly.

"What? Why not? I have to!" Melody said.

"Nope. Not happening," Matthew told her. "If you think Tex would ever forgive me, or any of us, for putting you in the middle of this clusterfuck, you're wrong. You'll stay here, where you'll be safe."

"If this Asher guy is as smart as Ryleigh says he is, he knows that's what John's friends will say. He obviously knows where I live, since he kidnapped us from our own street. He's aware that there's no way anyone would let me go to that drop. What better way to circle back around and snatch me out from under your noses while you're all occupied at the damn Sugar Shack?"

"Shit. She has a point," Baker growled. Honest-to-God growled. In any other situation, Melody might've found it hot.

"What if we turn the tables on him?" Beth asked. "He knows we aren't going to bring a billion dollars in cash to the drop. He probably won't even be there. If Ryleigh's right, he just wants to fuck with Melody...and Tex. So you guys can hit any possible places where Ryleigh thinks Tex might be stashed, while Melody goes to The Sugar Shack...not alone," she added quickly. "Cade could go with her. Or maybe there's another one of Tex's friends who could go with her."

"I'll call the guys," Matthew said quickly.

"The guys?" Melody asked.

"Yeah. Abe, Cookie, Dude, Mozart, and Benny. Hurt and Cutter will stay home to look after the families, just in case this Rook guy decides to branch out with his asshole-ness."

"I'm sure they have stuff going on," Melody protested, but deep down, she knew she'd feel a hell of a lot better with Matthew's SEAL team there with her.

"I'll call Truck and my dad too. *No one* fucks with Truck," Annie said with a shit-eating grin on her face. "He and I can team up to check out any places

Ryleigh comes up with, and Fletch can stay with you and the rest of the guys, Melody."

"How are you going to get her to The Sugar Shack without this Rook guy seeing a vehicle full of six former special forces guys?" Jodelle asked.

"The more I think about this, the more I think Ryleigh is right. Rook never intended to meet Melody at that abandoned factory. But for the one percent chance he *is* there, we'll only put one of our guys in the vehicle with her," Matthew said. "He'll be crouched down in the front seat next to her. The others will fan out and infiltrate the factory grounds and building. If anyone's there, they'll find him— them—and wait for the right moment to take them out."

For the first time, Melody began to feel a bit more optimistic. "And the money?" she asked.

"It won't be necessary either way. If Rook is there, we'll take him down. If no one shows up, the money still isn't needed," Baker said.

"Why hasn't he called?" Melody asked. That detail had been bugging her. "Why pass the message about the money through that kid? If he truly wants me to suffer, wouldn't he call to gloat that he has John? To hurt him more while I'm listening live?"

"Because he knows he could be tracked that way,"

Beth said. "He knows what Tex can do with anything electronic, and probably figures he's got friends who can do the same thing. So he's avoiding any places with cameras, or sending emails or texts, or calling. He's trying to go old school, thinking he can stay under the radar that way."

"Idiot," Ryleigh muttered through the phone. "I'm gonna start searching for spots where Rook could stash Tex. I'll be in touch. Oh, and by the way, we passed nine hundred million in donations."

Melody gasped. "Holy shit."

"You and Tex will have to figure out what to do with the money when he comes home," Ryleigh told her.

"Give it back!" Melody said without hesitation. "We don't need it."

"Not so fast," Baker said. "Think about what Tex could do with that kind of cash. Trackers, foundations for the missing, training for police departments...the possibilities are endless."

He wasn't wrong. "But won't people want their money back, once they find out it wasn't needed after all?" she asked.

"Some, maybe. But I'm thinking the people who donated money did so not thinking they'd see it again. They did so because of Tex's legacy. Because of all the good he's done in the world," Jodelle said gently.

Maybe because it was Jodelle who'd said the words—a woman Melody had only recently met, someone she hadn't even known existed until this fucked-up situation, who was with a man who reminded her a hell of a lot of John—but Melody seriously began to consider all the good a billion dollars could do for the missing and exploited of the world.

"I can help you figure out where to donate, if you go that route," Ryleigh said from the phone speaker. "I've had lots of experience with that kind of thing myself."

"There will be time for all of that later," Matthew said. "We have until tomorrow at eleven to come up with a plan."

Melody still had no idea if John was truly all right or not. That shot she'd heard on the tape had shaken her to the core. But now that they had some semblance of a plan, she felt a little lighter deep down. The possibility that she might soon be reunited with her husband had her wishing time would pass more quickly. She wanted it to be eleven o'clock tomorrow night, right now. So she could get John back.

Of course, she had a feeling it wouldn't be as easy as she hoped. That whoever had John wanted to make them both suffer for as long as possible. But he'd underestimated the stubbornness of the SEALs, Deltas, Green Berets—Annie—and John's friends. They'd never give up trying to find him and get him back alive.

"Hang in there, honey. We're coming for you."

CHAPTER 10

TEX SAT IN THE DARK, that damn music continuing unabated, and once again cautiously probed the wound in his calf. It hurt like a motherfucker, but he thought the bleeding had finally stopped. Of course, that wouldn't do him any good if he got an infection. The thought of losing his other leg made him almost sick to his stomach.

Then again, he had no doubt that Melody wouldn't give a fig if he had one leg, one arm, or no arms. All she'd care about was him coming home alive.

Tex lay on his back and stared into the dark. He couldn't see a damn thing, but he didn't want to close his eyes. He racked his brain yet again, trying to figure out who could be behind this. He'd pissed off his share of people over the years, but he'd never felt as if he was in danger.

There was that time he'd crossed the New York Mafia, but he was fairly certain he'd managed to smooth things over there. It wasn't as if he'd meant to send the cops straight into a huge gun-running scheme. All he was trying to do was bring home a missing teenager.

He'd also run afoul of the drug cartels in Mexico, after that thing with Khloe Moore and Raiden Walker down in Virginia, but he was under the impression that no one liked Pablo Garcia that much anyway. Thought he was a hot-headed, arrogant asshole. And considering how much time he'd done in prison in America, he didn't have many contacts left south of the border when he'd been taken down for good.

Other situations flitted through Tex's brain as he did his best to figure out who he'd angered enough to put him in this situation. And not only that—who was smart enough to pull it off. That was probably the better question.

Try as he might, Tex couldn't come up with anyone from his past who stood out. But what this situation had done was hammer home that he needed to be far more vigilant about his and his family's safety. He frequently worked with the worst of humanity, and he hated that there had been blowback. The only consolation was that the blowback had been toward him. Yes, Melody had been caught up in this hell, but he was more relieved than he could say that she wasn't being held captive alongside him.

If his captor had *truly* wanted to torture him, that would've done it.

In fact, letting his wife go would be the man's downfall. Melody was smart and tough as hell. She was probably banged up and hurt—which made Tex's belly swirl in agitation—but she'd most certainly called in the troops. And while she didn't know everyone he'd worked with in the past, his friends would know who to call.

The first person she probably called was Wolf.

Thoughts of his old friend made Tex smile. Thinking back to when he'd helped Wolf find his then almost-girlfriend made the smile fade. Caroline had been through some shit, but like Melody—like a hell of a lot of women he'd helped over the years— she was way tougher than even she could've imagined.

Wolf probably took the first flight across the country to be at Melody's side. He'd protect her and his girls, of that Tex had no doubt. He wondered who Wolf would choose to contact. Penelope? The soldier turned firefighter from San Antonio? Trigger and his team of Deltas? Maybe Phantom and his fellow former SEALs? Maybe even Ghost and his Deltas. Most of the men he called his friends were no longer active duty, but they were no less badass. There was no shortage of men and women who Tex thought wouldn't hesitate to offer their assistance.

But if there was one person out there who could figure out this entire fucked-up situation...it was Ryleigh Lodge.

The kid—okay, she wasn't exactly a kid, but she was much younger than Tex, which made her a kid in his eyes—was a fucking genius. Way smarter than Tex. She'd been dealt a shit hand when it came to family, but she'd found a new family on The Refuge out in New Mexico. Surely Wolf would think of her. He'd met her recently, when he and Caroline went out to The Refuge, and they'd been embroiled in a shitshow of epic proportion.

Ryleigh could hack into his computer and figure out who the most likely suspects were in regard to his kidnappers. And Tex had no problem with her getting into his files either. The woman had hacked into countless government databases and could probably launch nuclear weapons at a push of a button on her keyboard.

But she was also as trustworthy a person as he'd ever met. And generous. He knew all about the money she'd stolen from her criminal of a father over the years, and how she was attempting to quietly give it all away. Beyond that, all she wanted was to be left alone. To live her life.

Thinking about his friends made Tex forget about his current situation for a while. Forget about the music blaring into his skull. Forget about the pain in his calf from being shot. Forget that he was as helpless as he'd ever been. Nude, locked in a box, starving, and pissing in a bucket.

He'd get through this because the alternative was unthinkable. He just needed to let his friends do their thing. And they would...because that's the kind of men and women they were. Honorable, loyal, and stubborn as all get out.

That last thought made him smile. Tex had seen a lot of bad shit in his life, but the good stuff made it all worth it. Like his Melody and his daughters. And his friends. He was blessed. This would end and life would go on...hopefully with him back at his family's side, a whole lot wiser and more cautious as he went about his daily business.

* * *

"Ryleigh and I found a few possibilities!" Beth announced as she burst through the basement door into the living room, making Melody jerk in fright where she was sitting on the couch, trying not to go out of her skin with nerves.

It was five o'clock the next afternoon, and they only had six hours until she was supposed to meet John's kidnapper at The Sugar Shack.

Relieved that at *last*, Ryleigh and Beth had some information for them, Melody turned toward the disheveled woman. She'd been holed up in the basement for the last twelve hours or so and looked as exhausted as Melody felt...and probably looked herself.

But she also looked smugly satisfied.

"We came up with three options that would make good places to stash someone you didn't want anyone else to know about," Beth went on. "I marked them on a map, come here," she ordered, heading toward the kitchen table.

Everyone immediately stood and crowded around the table as Beth spread out a map of the area.

"Here's where we are, the town of Washington,"

she said, pointing to Melody's neighborhood. "And here's where Rook's mom lives, just north of town. And lastly, here's The Sugar Shack. It's about ten miles east of Rook's house. Between those two spots are the three places we think would make perfect places to hole up.

"First up, here. It's an old gas station along a rarely used road. It used to have a lot of traffic, but then the interstate was built, making it obsolete. There's a large freezer in there that could easily hold a prisoner. It's obviously not a freezer anymore, as there's no electricity going to the place, but there aren't any windows and it could be locked from the outside. Rook could stash Tex there and head off to live his normal life, without fear that Tex could escape while he was gone.

"Secondly, there's an old house that went through foreclosure and was never bought from the bank, and it's been left to rot. There's a barn behind it, with weeds and vines making it almost inaccessible. The driveway to get out there is at least half a mile long, so it's very remote.

"And lastly—probably the most unlikely spot, but we thought we should mention it because we have no idea what this Rook guy is thinking—is an old trap house in a pretty crappy neighborhood. There are people still living in the area, but they mostly keep to themselves. Most of the inhabitants are on the sex registry, so they want nothing to do with cops and bringing any kind of attention to themselves."

"Which do you think is the best likelihood for where Tex could be stashed?" Matthew asked.

Beth pressed her lips together and straightened from the table. She shrugged a little. "Ry and I talked about it, and the smartest place would be the gas station. That freezer is a ready-made cell. There's no way Tex could be able to get out of there on his own. The old house is our second guess, although from viewing the satellite images, it doesn't look as if anyone has been out there in a long time. But that could be exactly what Rook *wants* it to look like. If he put Tex out there, secured him properly and left him, there wouldn't be much of a footprint of anyone being there.

"The most risky would be that house in the sex registry neighborhood. True, most people wouldn't call the cops because of their backgrounds, but that's not to say *no one* would. All it would take is one phone call and the entire plan could backfire. And Rook's too smart for that."

Matthew's cell vibrated with a text and he glanced at it. "The guys are here," he announced.

Melody smiled gratefully. As shitty as this situation was, she couldn't wait to see Abe, Cookie, Mozart, Dude, and Benny again. She'd missed them a lot, and mentally, she planned a trip out to California once John was back home and healed from his ordeal, so they could see all their women too.

Matthew went to the door and opened it, then the room was suddenly even more full than it was already.

Melody smiled broadly at the familiar faces as they filed in and immediately headed for her. They each gave her a long but gentle hug, mindful of her broken arm, and said how sorry they were about the situation.

She was speechless. There was so much Melody *wanted* to say, but she was suddenly overwhelmed and couldn't find the words. That these men had dropped everything to come to her side when she and John needed them the most was unbelievable.

Now that she really thought about it, she probably should've called that detective and informed him of what Ryleigh had found. Informed him about the supposed money drop and asked if he could provide security for her while she went out to The Sugar Shack.

But she hadn't...because she didn't really trust the man. She was sure he was competent at what he did, but this was her husband she was talking about. She couldn't afford any mistakes because his life was on the line. She trusted Matthew, and Baker, and John's friends. And most of all, she trusted the five newcomers with not only *her* life, but John's. If she went out there to the abandoned factory, and John was there, she wanted and needed these men at her side, and no one else.

"Thank you for coming," she finally managed to croak out.

"Nowhere else we'd be."

"Of course."

"We love you both."

"This is what friends do."

"This fucker is going down."

Melody couldn't help but chuckle at Dude's last comment. He was normally pretty stoic. She knew he was a Dominant, she and Cheyenne had talked enough for her to know the couple's sexual preferences were pretty...intense. He was all about taking charge. Also, everything about Dude screamed honorable. He took it as a personal offense when women were assaulted or battered. He'd no sooner hurt a woman than he'd lose control while on a mission. His entire life was about control, and right now, Melody needed his stability. His control. Because it felt like she had none.

"What's the plan?" Abe asked.

Before Matthew could speak, however, there was another knock at the door.

Turning, Melody saw a huge man enter her house through the unlocked front door the former SEALs had just used. He was one of the tallest men she'd ever seen, and he wore a scowl, which accented the gnarly scar on the side of his face. He was muscular on top of that. This was definitely a man she wouldn't want to come across in a dark alley... not that she was spending much time in dark alleys anyway.

Luckily, she knew exactly who the newcomer was. She'd met him once, maybe twice. So she wasn't freaking out that a badass scary-looking stranger had just walked into her house.

Before she could greet the man, Annie let out a loud whoop. "Trucker!" she screamed, making a beeline toward him.

Truck—Melody was sure he had a proper name, but she couldn't remember it at the moment—

grinned a lopsided grin and opened his arms as Annie threw herself into them.

"It's so good to see you, Sprite!" he told her, hugging her tightly.

"Same!" the woman exclaimed, smiling up at Truck. "I'm a little sad that Fletch couldn't come as well, but with Emily in the hospital with appendicitis, he didn't feel as if he could leave her. Trust me, I think it's killing him not to be here, but it's probably for the better, because he still thinks of me as a little kid who used to like to ride around the yard in that tank you guys made me."

They smiled at each other, then, as if they both remembered where they were and why, they turned toward Melody with all traces of amusement wiped off their faces.

"Are you okay?" Truck asked Melody gruffly, eyeing the cast on her arm.

"As well as I can be," she answered honestly. "Better, now that all you guys are here and we have somewhere to look for John."

Truck glanced around at the men. "What's the plan?"

Melody couldn't help but smile a little at that. He sounded exactly like Abe did a few moments ago.

These were men of action…which she fully approved of.

Matthew gave Truck a quick rundown of what Beth and Ryleigh had learned about who might be behind the kidnapping, and the possible locations of where John could be.

"I'm thinking most of my team will go with Melody to The Sugar Shack. I'm betting no one shows up when she gets there, but just in case, I want to make sure she's covered. Tex would have my ass if she got hurt while under our protection," Matthew said.

Melody was more than all right with that plan. She was grateful she wasn't being left out of tonight's activities altogether. She was well aware that everyone would've preferred that she stayed right where she was—safe at home—but since the kidnapper specifically ordered her to be the one to bring the money to the secluded location, no one wanted to do anything other than what was requested, just in case the kidnapper did show up.

"Baker and Cade can check out the abandoned gas station, I'll head to the farmhouse with Dude, and, Truck, you and Annie can check out the house in the sketchy neighborhood. If that's all right with everyone?"

Everyone nodded their agreement.

"Beth, if you or Ryleigh come up with any more intel that points to one location or another, or even makes you think Tex is nowhere near here anymore, call me immediately. I'll relay the info to the others."

"Okay, but that won't be necessary. Not really. I mean, as long as everyone has their phones on them, Ryleigh can text everyone at the same time. Make sure the intel gets sent out as fast as possible."

"Right, of course she can," Matthew said with a nod. Then he turned to the room in general once more. "Everyone put your phones on silent. The last thing anyone needs is a ping or chime alerting Rook or any other scumbag to our presence. We have a few hours before we need to head out. Melody, why don't you lie down, see if you can get some rest."

Melody snorted. That wasn't happening. She was ready to go *now*. She didn't want to wait for eleven o'clock to roll around. But she also knew the cover of darkness was important for the others as they searched for John. Yes, they were all special ops, but they wanted to be sure they had the upper hand. No one had forgotten that there had been five people involved in her and John's kidnapping. They could call for more backup, there were plenty of people out there with military experience that would be happy to fly in and help, but they didn't want to wait until tomorrow to make a move. So they were compromising by splitting up the man-and woman-power they had now, by waiting until it was dark to make their move.

She supposed she should be more nervous than she was. Should've wanted someone else, most likely Annie, to pretend to be her and go to The Sugar Shack in her stead. But she needed to do this. Needed to have some role in getting John back. Even if it turned out she was on a fool's errand, and the kidnapper had no intention of meeting her at the deserted factory, it still felt as if she was helping. And she certainly wasn't scared. Not with Abe, Cookie, Benny, and Mozart with her.

"I can't sleep," she told Matthew firmly.

He nodded as if he expected that response.

"I want to visit with everyone a bit. It's been a while since I've seen you guys," Melody said, glancing at the newcomers.

Abe came over and put his arm around her shoulders, giving her a side hug.

Surprisingly, the next couple of hours went by quickly. It was nice to catch up with the SEALs from California, and Truck. But when ten o'clock rolled around, and Matthew announced it was time to head out, she was more than ready.

Abe and Cookie had put every duffel bag and suitcase they could find in the house into the back of Melody's car. Just in case someone was at the abandoned factory, they wanted it to look like Melody had some money with her. That she was complying with the demands of the kidnapper. The duffels were filled with towels and the suitcases were empty. Melody had been coached to pretend they were heavy as she removed them from the car...if things came to that.

The instructions they'd received for the money drop had been sparse at best. Just secondhand from the clerk at the gas station.

The plan was for Cookie to be in the car with her and the others to precede them, park a ways from the factory, and fan out, searching the grounds. If someone was there, they'd keep an eye on them until the person made themselves known to Melody when she arrived. Cookie would crouch down on the passenger side of her car to protect her if shit hit the fan.

Baker and Cade would head to the gas station as planned, to check out the freezer and see if that's where John had been stashed.

Matthew and Dude would go the farmhouse...
again, parking a safe distance away so as not to alert
anyone who might be watching that someone was
coming, and once again, see if they could find John.

Lastly, Annie and Truck would go to the sketchy
neighborhood. They wouldn't need to park as far
away as the other two groups, since it was a popu-
lated community. But that also made it less likely
that John was there. Even with the inhabitants being
mostly sex offenders and other men and women
who'd been on the wrong side of the law at one time
or another, the chances of someone seeing something suspicious and calling the police was higher
than at the other two locations.

Melody hoped like hell Ryleigh and Beth were
right, and John was at one of the three locations.
Because the alternative was unthinkable. If he'd been
transported out of the area, it would be even harder
to find him. And without the kidnapper communi-
cating with Melody, telling her what he wanted, she
wasn't sure what the outcome of this shitshow
would be.

She did know she was ready for it to end. She
couldn't fathom having to go another day, week,
month, year, without knowing where her husband
was. Couldn't imagine having to tell Hope that her

daddy was "lost." The agony of not knowing where he was or what he was going through was hard enough after just a few days. Melody literally couldn't imagine what it would feel like for weeks or more to go by and not know.

She had confidence in John's friends. She'd heard him say more than once how talented Ryleigh was. How John thought she was the better hacker. Melody wasn't sure she believed him, but just him saying that was huge. It meant her husband had an immense amount of respect for the young woman. She had to be right. She simply had to.

Melody hugged each and every one of the men and women in the room, thanking them for being there, for doing what needed to be done to find John.

And she wasn't surprised when everyone blew off her thanks. Saying it was what friends did. And what John had done for years for all of them.

"It goes without saying that if you find Tex, the first thing you need to do is contact one of us," Matthew said sternly. "No going in by yourself. None of us will be that far away, we can be at your location in minutes. Tex's best chance to make it out of this without Rook, or whoever the kidnapper is, killing him before he can be rescued is if we work together. Understood?"

Everyone nodded their assent. The words *killing him* echoed in Melody's brain. They couldn't get this close to rescuing John to lose him at the last second.

"And if there is someone at The Sugar Shack, let us know as soon as possible," Matthew told his team. "From the satellite pictures Ryleigh sent, it would be an excellent place to interrogate whoever is there to collect the money."

Melody wasn't shocked by his words, or even turned off by them. She almost wished someone *would* be there. If the men around her could get someone to tell them where John was, she didn't care how the information was obtained. As far as she was concerned, the ends would justify the means, and the kidnapper brought on whatever was coming his way by what he'd done.

"Let's do this. Remember...protect Tex at all costs," Matthew reminded the group. "We have no idea what shape he'll be in if we find him. Not after all this time. If that means letting Rook or anyone else go, that's fine. He won't escape. We'll get him one way or another. There's nowhere he can hide with Ryleigh and Beth on his case. And when Tex recovers, he won't rest until he sees his kidnapper dead or behind bars. Understand?"

This time the nods and affirmative responses were a little less enthusiastic. Melody understood. The last thing she wanted was the man who'd kidnapped her and John out there free, plotting and planning to do it again. She didn't want to live her life in a bubble, constantly looking over her shoulder. But Matthew was right. If letting the bad guy or bad guys go meant protecting John and freeing him, that's what needed to happen. John was the most important thing here. Period.

Caroline, Jodelle, and Beth hugged her tightly, wishing her luck, before Melody headed out the door. She was more than ready to do this. It beat sitting around the house worrying and wondering what was happening to John. She hoped like hell whatever happened in the next hour or so would end this nightmare once and for all.

CHAPTER 11

TEX HAD no idea if it was day or night. No one had opened the box he'd been locked in for...hours? Days? He was hungry and thirsty. He'd finished the water that had been left for him quite a while ago. His lips were chapped, his calf hurt like hell, and he couldn't see it to assess the damage done by the bullet. He wasn't happy with how hot his leg felt though. And he could no longer stand. He'd tried.

Shooting pains had dropped him on his ass the last time he'd tried to grin and bear it and put weight on his leg. As much as he hated to admit it, his kidnapper had effectively taken Tex's ability to escape off the table. If the men returned and left the door to his box wide open, Tex wouldn't even be able to hop.

Gritting his teeth, he vowed that if the chance arose, he'd *crawl* to safety if that's what it took. He wouldn't give up, no matter how weak he'd become. The only easy day was yesterday, that was the SEAL motto, and he'd been in worse situations than this in the past. He simply had to hang on one more week, day, hour, minute.

The asshole who'd taken him wanted something. Tex had yet to figure out exactly what that was. But he'd been taken for a reason, just as Melody had been let go for a reason. He'd racked his brain over and over trying to figure out who the man was...the one who'd shot him on tape. By now, Melody had probably received the recording. And if she'd listened to it, she was probably a complete mess. Not that he'd blame her.

He remembered the audio they'd received when Caroline was taken. The asshole responsible had recorded himself beating the crap out of her. How hard that was for Wolf to listen to. Hell, it had been difficult for Tex to hear, and he wasn't in love with the woman. He hated that Melody was in the same situation now. He prayed she'd understand that the shot hadn't been fatal. If she thought he was dead...

He couldn't finish the thought. It was unfathomable. If the roles were reversed, Tex wasn't sure he'd be able to function. But his Melody was a rock. She'd power through any emotions the tape evoked and she'd plan. Or at least help his friends plan.

For the first time in his life, all Tex could do was lie there and wait. He couldn't participate in rescuing himself. Well...that wasn't exactly true. He could stay alive. That was his job right now. To keep breathing. To keep his heart beating. It was a weird position to be in, especially for someone who was used to being at the heart of missions to find people.

But he wasn't embarrassed.

Wasn't ashamed.

That was victim-blaming behavior. And he hadn't done a damn thing to put himself into this situation. Sometimes bad guys had the upper hand. But his kidnapper's time would come. He'd go down, along with everyone who was helping him. If not by his own hand, by the many men and women Tex knew around the world.

No one would rest until they found Tex...dead or alive...and made the people responsible pay.

Believing in that, bone deep, was helping Tex cope. He wasn't really alone. Physically, yes...but the knowledge that people were right that second turning over every rock and checking every scrap of digital information for those responsible for abducting him, was what kept him going.

Tex took a deep breath.

Then another.

He ignored the way his belly cramped.

The way he felt his heart felt like it beat in his calf.

The phantom pains in his missing leg that he hadn't felt for years.

Help was coming.

He just had to be patient.

ANNIE FLETCHER clenched and unclenched her fists in anticipation and to make sure they stayed limber. She was *more* than ready for this. Making it through training to become a Green Beret had already been the most difficult thing she'd ever done in her life. If it hadn't been her instructors trying to make her quit, it was her fellow soldiers. She could more than handle a few lowlife kidnappers.

Many people didn't even believe women should be in combat, let alone become special forces soldiers. But screw that. She'd showed them all. And one day she would be in charge of her own platoon.

She'd have soldiers who respected her and her abilities. She'd be the best leader they'd ever known.

There were a few people who'd always believed in her. Her parents, of course. They'd been behind her one hundred percent. Telling her that she could do anything, be anything.

Frankie…the boy she'd loved since she was seven years old. She was going to marry him someday, but first she'd needed to prove to herself, and the world, that she could make it as a special forces soldier, just like her dad and their friends.

Speaking of which, every single one of her dad's former teammates—they were all retired now—were also her cheerleaders. They'd tirelessly gone through obstacle courses with her, grilled her on the stuff she had to memorize, and generally lifted her up when she was feeling down about the path she was on. Truck and his wife, Mary, had been her staunchest supporters. Sending care packages and emails, always there when she needed someone to bitch to about everything she was dealing with.

And then there was Tex.

She hadn't seen him in years, but she still remembered how much of a badass he was at her parents' wedding reception, when some…*uninvited guests* showed up. She'd always admired him and trusted his advice. When she'd been on the verge of quitting the Green Beret program, it was Tex who'd talked her out of it.

The man had also given her many trackers over the years, and she'd had no qualms whatsoever in keeping one of them on her person at all times. Tex was like her own personal guardian angel, and there was a huge comfort in knowing he could see her whereabouts any time of the day and would always be there if she needed him, no ifs, ands, or buts about it.

So when she'd heard he'd been kidnapped, Annie hadn't hesitated in requesting—no, demanding leave, so she could get to Pennsylvania and offer any assistance she could. She was no computer genius, but she was more than capable of using the skills she'd learned over the years to infiltrate a hideout and both rescue and protect Tex, if it came down to it.

She was extremely grateful to Wolf for pairing her with Truck tonight. No one knew if any of the three spots Ryleigh and Beth had come up with would prove viable. If Tex would be found at any of them. But she prayed that if he was...it was at the house she and Truck were going to check out.

It didn't seem likely. Who would stash a kidnap

victim in the middle of an active neighborhood, where anyone might overhear or see what was going on? True, it wasn't likely the neighbors would call the cops, as they weren't exactly upstanding citizens and most had their own history with authority figures. But the chance wasn't a total zero.

Truck parked his rental SUV behind a sketchy-looking gas station at the entrance to the neighborhood. "I'm gonna go in and tell them not to fuck with my car," he said.

Annie wanted to roll her eyes. As if telling someone not to mess with his shit would make them *not* mess with his shit. But, then again, Truck was pretty intimidating. If it wasn't his six-foot seven-inch height, it was the scar on his cheek that pulled his lips down into a perpetual scowl.

She didn't give a rat's ass about his scar; her dad and others in his circle still loved to tell the story of the first time she'd met Truck, when she was a little kid, and how she'd put her tiny palm over his scar and asked if it hurt when it happened.

"Stay here," Truck ordered, before climbing out of the SUV and slamming the door behind him.

Annie did as he asked, simply because she was going over different scenarios in her head as to how the next few minutes might go. What they might say if they ran into anyone while checking out the place Ryleigh and Beth had pinpointed as a potential stash house. How they could gain entry.

What they'd do if they actually found Rook or Tex or anyone else inside.

Truck was back in less than a minute, and Annie got out of the passenger side of the vehicle. She checked her pistol, making sure it was secure in its holster at the small of her back. Then she checked her KA-BAR knife in the sheath strapped to her thigh. She pulled out the pair of night vision goggles she'd packed at the last minute, just in case. And lastly, she patted the small knife tucked into a pocket she'd sewn onto the strap of her sports bra. She'd practiced throwing it until she could hit a target dead center at fifteen feet or less.

Without a word, she and Truck faded into the trees surrounding the parking lot of the gas station. Truck led the way, walking silently through the trees and underbrush. For such a large man, he could move as quietly as any deadly predator. Annie watched him carefully, using this as a learning experience for herself as much as a potential rescue mission. She always had more to learn, and who better to learn from than the best of the best?

They passed a couple of houses with loud music

coming from inside but didn't slow down. They interrupted what Annie assumed had to be a drug deal, but when she and Truck didn't even look twice, the two men continued what they were doing. This wasn't a neighborhood for children, and thankfully, she didn't see signs that any lived there. The smell of pot was thick in the air and there was a feeling of anticipation that felt unnatural and sinister. As if everyone who lived there was simply waiting for something bad to happen.

As they approached their target, Truck led the way around to the backside of the supposedly abandoned house...

Except there was a light coming from inside. It wasn't bright, but it was a light all the same.

"Truck," Annie said, reaching out and holding onto his arm with an iron grip.

"I see it," he said in an almost silent tone.

He pulled out his phone and shot off a quick text. Annie could only assume he was getting a hold of Wolf.

"I told him to be ready. That we hadn't found anything yet. It could be a squatter, someone shooting up, or someone having sex with a prostitute," Truck said in that same deathly quiet voice.

Annie nodded. But every nerve ending in her

body was telling her that whoever was in that house wasn't doing any of the things Truck had mentioned. Tex was in there. Her gut was screaming that she was right.

"I'll go around the back. Check the windows," she told him. She hadn't perfected that toneless whisper he did so well, but he didn't seem perturbed that her voice was a touch louder than his.

"All right. If you find anything, text Wolf, then me."

Annie nodded and pulled out her phone. She pulled up the messaging app and clicked on Wolf's name. She typed out, *he's here*, but didn't send it. If she found Tex, all she had to do was reopen the app and click send. Not waste more time typing out the message.

"We'll go in together if he's there," Truck continued. "You from the back, me from the front. If shit goes sideways, protect Tex. Get him out of there."

"What about you?" Annie asked. She felt a fire inside, knowing that Truck was trusting her with Tex's life. He could've easily tasked her with subduing whoever had that light on in the house, but instead he was asking her to save Tex. That meant the world to her. His trust and belief in her abilities made her forget every instructor who told her she'd never make it. Every fellow applicant who said she'd never be a green beret special forces soldier.

"It's been a while since I've done this, but no one fucks with Tex."

It wasn't really an answer, but then again, it was. "We need answers," Annie reminded Truck.

"I know."

Mentally, Annie shrugged. She didn't give a fuck what Truck did with whoever was in that house. Her only concern was Tex. She had no doubt Truck could take care of himself. Even if there was more than one person in the house, even if the kidnapper had a whole contingent of bad guys in there with him, having a damn orgy or something. Truck would deal with them.

"Be careful," he said, right before they split apart. "Fletch would never forgive me if I got his baby hurt."

Annie rolled her eyes. "Don't worry about me. Worry about you...old man," she teased.

Truck grinned at her, then turned serious once more. "Time to get our friend back."

"A SEAL never leaves a SEAL behind," Annie recited. Neither she nor Truck were SEALs, but Tex was. And they weren't leaving him behind. Not a chance in hell.

Truck faded into the darkness. One second he was there, and the next, Annie was standing alone. It was almost uncanny how silent Truck was, considering his size, but she had no time to contemplate how he did it.

Doing her best to stay in the shadows, Annie crept toward the back of the house in question. The weeds and grass were long on the backside of pretty much every house in the neighborhood, providing the perfect coverage. Moving quickly, she made her way directly behind the house that should've been abandoned. No light came through any of the windows at the back of the house. Pulling the night-vision goggles over her eyes so she could see in the dark, Annie moved like a shadow to the first window.

Peering in, she saw what looked like a bedroom. She could just make out boxes stacked up on a crooked bed frame. There was trash strewn about the space and what looked like feces on the floor as well. She didn't stop to wonder if it was human or animal. Shit was shit.

Moving to the only other window, she attempted to look inside. To her surprise, all she saw was the faint reflection of her face staring back her. Blinking in confusion, Annie realized this room had some sort of curtains over the window.

Her gut stirring with nerves and excitement—because there was absolutely no reason for curtains to be closed in an empty house, especially one that looked as if it was used by anyone who happened to need a place for their nefarious activities—she pulled out her phone.

She quickly sent the text she'd typed out to Wolf. She was certain, even without seeing absolute proof, that Tex was on the other side of those curtains. She'd bet her reputation as a green beret on it. She then sent a text to Truck.

Yes.

One word. That's all she took the time to say, but Truck would understand. She was pretty sure he was already thinking the same thing she was—that Tex was there.

Annie had some options here. Break the glass and alert whoever was in the front of the house that someone was possibly trying to rescue their captive, making all their lives more difficult. Or cross her fingers and hope against hope that before the curtains were pulled tightly across the window...whoever had done, so hadn't bothered to check the lock.

Holding her breath, Annie pushed up on the window.

To her amazement and delight, it moved up.

Idiots! The window was unlocked!

On the heels of that thought was worry. If the window was unlocked, and Tex was inside, he could've gotten out at any time. Even if he had been bound, or hurt, he was a SEAL. Yes, he was old—her dad would kick her ass if he ever got wind that she'd thought of Tex as *old*, because he wasn't far from his age—but there's no way he would've simply sat around waiting for rescue if he could've gotten out himself.

But the fact that he *hadn't* gotten out already wasn't a good sign. Even she knew that. He was probably incapacitated in some way. Which made her want to vomit, but she forced those feelings away. She had a job to do here and she wasn't going to fail.

Annie doubted her instincts for the first time and regretted sending those texts until she was completely sure Tex was inside. It was too late now. The only thing she could do was move aside the curtain and see for herself if her gut, and training, was right.

She went to push the curtains aside and realized

they were somehow attached on the sides and where they met in the middle. She pushed harder and realized they were taped to the window frame. But the bottom wasn't secured like the sides were.

Moving as fast as she dared while still attempting to not make a sound, Annie peeled the tape off of one side of the curtains, away from the wall, and looked inside the room for the first time.

She was confused. It was empty. No trash on the floor like the other room. No boxes. No furniture except for a chair in the very middle of the space. As she stared at it a bit longer, Annie could see zip-ties hanging off the back slats.

Motherfucker. She hadn't been wrong. Tex was here. Or he had been at one time. Likely secured to the very chair she was looking at. The door to the room was shut and she took the opportunity to push herself up into the window and slide into the room. Crouching under the window, Annie paused, waiting. Listening.

To her confusion, she heard music coming from somewhere. It was faint, but now that she was inside the room, much more clear than when she was on the other side of the curtains outside.

And now that she was inside, she could also see

what she hadn't before. Someone had built a false wall.

No, it wasn't a wall. It was a box.

Her eyes widening, Annie moved without thinking about the consequences. She wasn't trying to be stealthy anymore, she was horrified at what she was seeing. The wood of the box had been painted black, which was why she hadn't immediately recognized what she was seeing. It blended into the darkness of the room. And also, now that she was right next to it, she could hear the music easier. It was coming from *inside* the box.

Fuck! She had *zero* doubt now. This was Tex's prison—and she was getting him the fuck out of there. But how to do so and not alert whoever was in the other room? They'd hear the music the second she opened the box.

A noise from outside the door had Annie spinning around, weapon in hand instinctively as she knelt and pointed it at the door. But seconds later, she realized whoever she heard wasn't anyone about to come rushing in.

That sound was Truck, fighting with whoever he'd encountered.

Now was her chance. While Truck was busy with whoever was on the other side of that door.

Holstering her pistol, Annie turned back to the box. There were two padlocks on the small door, holding it shut at the top and bottom. Piece of cake.

Reaching into one of the cargo pockets of her pants, she pulled out the lock-picking tools she always carried and had learned to use almost as easily as others used an everyday key. She made quick work of the first lock, then knelt to pick the second. Twenty seconds had probably passed, which felt like an eternity for Annie.

She wanted to make sure Truck was all right, help him if need be, but her responsibility was Tex. Protecting him and getting him the hell out of there. Truck would never forgive her if she didn't do her job.

Wrenching the door open, the music that was barely audible from outside the box seemed especially loud now. Wincing, Annie strained to see into the darkness. There were no lights inside the small area, and it took her a moment to understand what she was seeing.

Tex.

He was lying on his side, curled into a ball at the back of the space. He was completely naked and was missing his prosthetic. But it was the fact that he didn't move when she opened the door that had Annie concerned.

She could see dark splotches on the floor and smell the bucket of waste that Tex had been using for his bodily needs. But she ignored those as she crouched slightly to step into the cell.

"Tex?" she whispered, but there was no response from the man on the floor. She realized as soon as she spoke that he wouldn't hear her over the sound of the music anyway. She didn't really need to be so quiet. No one would hear a damn thing going on in this room, just as Tex wouldn't be able to hear anything going on outside of it.

Hatred rose up within Annie. The sight of her idol lying motionless and injured made her want to fucking kill those who'd done this to him.

"Protect Tex. That's your job," she muttered to herself.

She needed to get him out of here. Away from this hell. Then she could do a medical assessment. See what needed to be done to help him.

Without hesitation, not thinking twice about his lack of clothes, Annie took a deep breath—regretting it instantly, as the air in this box wasn't exactly fresh —and leaned over the larger-than-life Tex. Except he wasn't larger than life at the moment. Even Annie could tell he'd lost weight during the days he'd been missing. Something else to hold those bastards accountable for.

As she'd done so many times before in training and in the hell that was green beret qualification, she hefted Tex over her shoulders in a fireman's carry, his head at one shoulder and his torso resting on her upper back, his leg dangling on her other side. He actually weighed less than the dummies and men she'd been required to prove she could carry while in training.

Annie cautiously moved out of the box. Her hands were full, and it would be difficult—not impossible, but difficult—to protect them both if someone burst into the room right about now. But the door stayed shut. Annie moved toward the window.

"Sorry about this, Tex," she said, before leaning out the window and basically dropping him onto the grass below. It worried her that he hadn't come to yet. She had no idea why, but she knew he wasn't dead. His body was warm. Almost *too* warm.

She quickly climbed out the window and once more picked up Tex and put him over her shoulders.

The relief that swept over her when she felt Tex

stir as she moved back toward the cover of the trees lining the neighborhood was immense.

"Tex?" she asked, in a tone that was louder than she'd like, but still only above a whisper. "It's Annie. I've got you. You're safe now."

"Annie?" the man over her shoulders croaked into her ear. The word was too loud. The music that had been blaring into that box had fucked with his hearing, and he probably had no idea how loud he was speaking.

Annie eased him to the ground and slammed her hand over his lips, frowning at him and shaking her head.

He nodded in understanding. Then said in a voice that was almost too low for her to hear, "Thank God they sent the best of the best." He'd obviously understood the need to be quiet, but was still unable to regulate his speech because his hearing was so messed up.

Regardless, Annie couldn't stop the grin from forming on her lips. Leave it to Tex to stroke her ego in the middle of his own damn rescue.

She thanked him using sign language, not wanting to risk anyone overhearing if she spoke.

To her delight—it shouldn't really have surprised

her, yet it did anyway—Tex signed back, *How's Melody?*

She began to respond, but gunfire erupted from the house they'd just left behind. Annie wasn't sure what was happening, and she didn't want Tex to be struck by a stray bullet. It would suck to be kidnapped and held captive for days, only to be shot accidentally during your rescue.

There was no way Annie was bringing Tex back to the gas station right now, as was her original plan. She wanted to make sure the area was safe. That no one was waiting in ambush for them. She'd just hunker down right here and wait for Truck, or Wolf, or someone to text her to give her the all clear. And she had no doubt that's what would happen when they couldn't find her or Tex in the house or immediate vicinity.

More shots sounded, and Annie crouched in front of Tex with her pistol out and pointed in the direction of the shots. Over her dead body was anyone taking Tex again. Not fucking happening.

Her attention was split between the direction of the house and her immediate surroundings. It wasn't likely anyone would be able to sneak up on her, but the possibility was there. She missed having someone at her six.

As soon as she had the thought, she felt her KA-BAR knife being slipped out of the sheath on her thigh. Since she heard Tex grunting with the effort it took to move, she knew it was him. Warmth shot through her. She'd just been wishing someone had her six, and there was Tex…having her six.

She'd thought he was too out of it. Too injured. Too weak to be able to be much help. What an idiot she was. Tex was a warrior through and through. The only way he'd be too weak was if he was dead, and even then she guessed he'd find a way to be of some assistance.

A minute or so passed, and neither Annie nor Tex moved. They were both at the ready, waiting for something to happen. When her phone vibrated in her pocket, it scared the hell out of Annie. She wanted to laugh at herself. Some special forces soldier she was…terrified by a damn cell phone.

Moving slowly, she reached with her free hand to her back pocket and pulled out her cell. Looking down, she saw a text from Truck.

All clear.

Relief swam through her veins. She had no idea if he was hurt, if Wolf and the others had shown up, or even if the person who'd kidnapped Tex had been taken into custody. But if Truck said the coast was clear, it was safe to get Tex some medical attention.

Annie debated for a beat on whether to go directly to the SUV or back to the house where Tex had been held prisoner. Truck helped by sending another text.

Meet you at the SUV.

Perfect.

Turning to Tex, Annie signed, *Truck says it's clear. We're going to the vehicle to get you some medical attention.*

Without missing a beat, Tex signed back, *Truck is here?*

Annie grinned and nodded. *And Wolf. And the rest of his crew. And Baker. And Beth and her husband.*

"Damn," Tex said out loud, his voice much more moderated. The time away from the blaring music had done him some good, and it looked like his hearing was returning to normal.

"Can you walk if I help?" Annie asked. She hadn't gotten a good look at his leg yet. She'd been more concerned about a tango coming through the trees to steal Tex back. It was also still dark, with only enough light to barely see each other in order to communicate via sign language.

"No."

Tex didn't look happy about his answer, but Annie was relieved he was being honest with her.

She nodded, put the pistol back in its holster at the small of her back, then stood. "You want to keep that?" she asked, nodding toward the knife Tex still held in his grasp.

"Yes."

"All right. Just don't accidentally stick me with it. It's fucking sharp," she told him.

Tex grinned. "Good girl."

She rolled her eyes. Leaning over, she picked up one of the men in the world she admired above all others and easily hefted him back onto her shoulders. "Hang on," she told him unnecessarily.

Moving quickly but silently—although not as silently as Truck could move—Annie headed back toward the gas station where they'd left the SUV. As she neared the area through the trees, she could see several people waiting for her.

Baker was there, as were Benny and Mozart. Truck wasn't anywhere that she could see. He must still be at the house. Just as she had the thought, she heard sirens in the distance…getting closer.

Baker saw her and Tex first. He peeled off from the others and came at them hard and fast. "Sitrep!" he barked.

"I'm okay," Tex answered before Annie could. "Gunshot in my calf that's infected. Dehydrated, beat all to shit, probably some bruised ribs that aren't hurting much right now, thanks to everything else. Hungry and weak as hell, but alive...thanks to Annie."

"I'll take him," Mozart said. He and Benny had followed the older man.

"No. I'm fine where I am," Tex said firmly.

Once again, warmth shot through Annie. Tex trusted her to finish what she started. She didn't need anyone to take over for her. She could carry Tex for at least another couple of miles if she had to. She'd trained for this kind of thing, and she was grateful he understood how disrespectful it would be if the men tried to take over.

"Tex? You know you're naked, right?" Benny asked, humor lacing his words.

"I am? Wow, thanks for letting me know," Tex said sarcastically.

"Fucking kidnappers," Mozart said under his breath.

"Took my leg too. I'm more pissed about that," Tex said, as if they were having a conversation over coffee or something. "If anyone can find it, I'd appreciate it. That thing wasn't cheap."

"On it," Baker said, his thumbs moving over the screen of his cell as they all walked toward the SUV.

"What happened at the house?" Annie asked, her curiosity getting the better of her, now that Tex was safe.

"Truck happened," Baker said, his lips twitching upward. "And it *was* Asher Rook, by the way. Thank fuck. Because the last thing I wanted was to go toe-to-toe with the fucking Mafia. I would've, but it's good that I don't have to. Asshole was sitting in the dark with only a small light illuminating the area, playing a fucking video game. As if he didn't have a human being locked in a box in the room behind him. He was so sure of himself, that he wouldn't get caught, that he was nonchalantly playing *This is War.*"

"Ballsy. Harley will be pissed when she hears that," Annie said, knowing exactly how the wife of one of her dad's Delta buddies would feel when she discovered the man who'd kidnapped Tex, had learned some of his tactics from the video game she'd helped design. It would infuriate her to no end.

"And the gunshots?" Tex asked. "Anyone hurt?"

"Rook had a pistol next to him, and when Truck kicked the door in, he picked it up and shot blindly," Baker informed them.

"Amateur," Mozart muttered.

"Missed by a mile," Benny agreed. "But it gave Truck a reason to shoot back. Asshole went down like a rock...crying like a baby, insisting he needed an ambulance."

Benny's words made Annie furious. "Oh, sure. He wants medical attention, but when he shot Tex, he didn't give a shit. What a sad excuse for a human being. What about the other men who helped with the kidnapping? None of them were there?"

"Nope, just Rook," Baker confirmed.

"Although the guys are there now, finding out who they were...names, addresses...everything they need to know to find them and make sure they pay for what they've done as well," Mozart said.

Just then, three police cars went flying past the gas station, their sirens blaring and the lights brightening up the area around the SUV momentarily before the area went dark once more.

"Shit. Are they gonna be in trouble?" Annie asked, staring after the cars. They could all hear the sirens turn into the neighborhood where Tex had been held.

"Nope. Truck was wearing a body camera. Self-defense," Baker said.

"But what about the interrogation?" Annie

insisted. There was no way Truck, Wolf, and the others wouldn't use any means necessary to get the intel they wanted. They might be retired, but they were the best of the best when it came to getting information out of people. She should know; she'd never been able to lie to her dad growing up. He was always able to get her to spill her guts when she did stupid shit like lie about where she was or who she was with.

Baker raised a brow. "You think they'd be dumb enough to record that?"

Annie chuckled. "Right. No."

"You guys think you can get me to the hospital sometime soon?" Tex asked, as if he was inquiring about the time.

"Fuck," Baker said, reaching for the handle on the backdoor of the SUV.

Annie felt just as guilty. She'd been so hungry for information about what went down at the house, she'd almost forgotten she was standing there holding a butt naked and wounded Tex.

She lowered one shoulder and managed to get him into the backseat. Benny stripped off his T-shirt and Tex draped it over his lap, nodding his thanks. Mozart ran around to get into the backseat next to Tex.

"Get in," Baker ordered Annie, motioning to the front seat with his head.

"I was going to go back to the house," she protested.

"Nope. You're going with us to the hospital. Truck wants to downplay your association with this as much as possible."

Annie nodded. It wasn't against any military rules for her to participate in the rescue of a civilian, but she didn't really want to bring any more attention to herself if she could help it. Life as a female green beret was tough enough as it was.

"Because you're still active duty. No one wants a spotlight on you."

That made sense. The last thing Annie wanted was the Army somehow using this against her. She had nothing to do with the shooting, so it shouldn't matter.

"Get in, Annie," Tex said firmly. "I need you to call Melody for me. Tell her that I'm okay. Be there with her when she gets to the hospital."

"Yes, Sir." She jogged around the SUV and got into the front seat. "What about you, Benny?" she asked.

"I'm headed to the house. I'll keep you all informed about what's happening." And then he was gone, disappearing into the same trees Annie had exited.

Baker got in behind the wheel of the SUV and pulled out from behind the gas station so fast, Annie had to grab the oh-shit handle above her head to keep from flying across the vehicle.

"Hang on back there. I'll have us at the hospital in three minutes," Baker informed everyone.

No one said anything for a long moment. Mozart was busy trying to assess Tex's bullet wound, which wasn't easy in the dark and with the way Baker was driving.

Tex's voice broke the silence surrounding the occupants.

"Thank you," he said, his voice full of emotion. "Feeling helpless is not something I've experienced much, and not something I want to experience again anytime soon."

"Holy fuck, did Tex just say thank you?" Baker asked under his breath.

Annie was thinking the same thing.

"I did. And I'll say it again. Thank you. I owe you all, huge."

"No, you don't," Mozart countered sternly. "You've helped countless people out of the same kinds of situations. You've helped me, Baker, Wolf...

and hundreds of other people. It's an honor to return the favor."

"Still, I feel as if I can't thank you all enough. Th—"

"*No*," Mozart interrupted. "No more. We'll start thinking this entire experience damaged you mentally if you go around thanking everyone all of a sudden."

Everyone in the car chuckled, including Tex.

"All right. Message received."

"Besides, if you attempted to thank everyone who sent you money, it would take you months...years even," Annie informed him.

"What do you mean?" he asked.

"There's a lot that happened since you were taken," Baker informed his fellow ex-SEAL. "Starting with the fact that the asshole who took you asked for a ransom of a billion dollars."

"The fuck?" Tex exclaimed.

"Yup. And once people heard you needed money, they sent it. In droves."

"Holy fucking shit," Tex swore again.

Annie did her best to stifle a giggle. Then she sobered. "You're so loved, Tex. People all over the country, the *world*, are aware of what you do for others. They wanted to return the favor. And when they heard *the* one and only Tex needed help, they were all too happy to do what they could."

"I don't want or need any of that money. It's going back," he said firmly.

"You'll hurt the feelings of the people who donated it," Mozart said easily.

"And for the record, Melody said the same thing," Baker added. "The two of you will have to figure out what to do with it. How to use it to help others who are taken from their loved ones. Soldiers. Sailors. The missing and exploited. Start a foundation. Scholarships. Wipe your ass with it. Whatever you want. But you can't give it back. Not after people were so eager to help the way you've helped them or their loved ones."

"But…a billion dollars?" Tex whispered.

"Talk to Ryleigh," Annie suggested. "She'll have some ideas on what you can do with it. From what I heard from Beth, she's made her fair share of charitable donations."

"Yeah, she has," Tex said absently.

"We're here," Baker announced as he pulled into the emergency entrance to the hospital.

"Think one of you can find me a wheelchair so Annie doesn't have to carry me in?" Tex asked. "I'm sure no one in there wants me to flash my naked ass at them."

Annie was so relieved to hear the Tex she knew and loved. When she first saw him in that box, she'd been terrified. Not so scared she couldn't do her job, but now that he was safe, the kidnapper caught, and Tex sounding more like himself, she could admit that this was the scariest thing she'd ever done, simply because it was someone she loved had been in danger. It was probably good experience. Would toughen her up in case something like this ever happened again—God forbid.

"Call Mel," Tex told Annie, as he transferred himself to the wheelchair Mozart had run into the ER to get and brought back to the car. "Tell her I'm fine. Upright, talking, ornery as ever."

"I will," she reassured him.

For a moment, she couldn't move as Mozart practically ran back into the ER, pushing Tex in front of him. She began to shiver as everything that happened finally sank in.

To her surprise, Baker's arm went around her shoulders, and he tugged her into him, giving her a tight, warm, comforting hug.

It was exactly what she needed at that moment.

Baker wasn't exactly the man she thought she'd *get* it from...but she should've known better. She'd seen him with Jodelle. How concerned he was for her, how attentive. He didn't miss much. And while some people might be embarrassed at their almost-break down, Annie wasn't. Her dad had told her time and time again that soldiers were people too. That she'd need to find a way to decompress after an intense mission.

"Thanks," she muttered into Baker's chest.

"Better?" he asked.

Annie nodded.

"Good. Now, get inside and call Melody like Tex ordered. I'll park and be inside in a moment."

Now *this* was the bossy Baker she'd gotten to know over the last few days.

She backed up and pulled out her cell, not bothering to watch Baker drive off in the SUV as she headed for the waiting room of the ER. It was about to get very crowded in there. Annie wondered if she should warn the staff how many people were about to descend on the hospital, but Melody answered the phone, distracting her.

"We found him. He's fine. Bossy and irritating as usual. He's here at the ER to get checked out. We'll see you soon and tell you everything when you get here."

Melody immediately burst out crying and couldn't talk.

Caroline took the phone from her, found out where they'd taken Tex, and said they'd be there soon.

After hanging up, Annie took a moment to close her eyes and simply breathe. The last few days had been horrific. But she felt like a changed person. Tex was all right. His family was okay. No one had been hurt. It was a good ending to a horrible nightmare.

Opening her eyes, she stepped forward, entering the chaotic emergency room lobby. There was still a lot of intel to learn regarding the entire situation, but Annie felt good about the outcome, her role in it, and about the path she was on in her life. This was what she wanted to do. Keep people safe. Protect. Rescue.

CHAPTER 12

TEX HAD no idea what time it was. Sometime in the afternoon, he thought. He'd been kept in the emergency room for hours. The doctors discussed surgery on his calf, but after cleaning it up and pumping him full of antibiotics for hours, they'd agreed to discharge him with the promise that if his leg got worse, he'd come back immediately.

His face hurt from all the beatings, a couple of his ribs were thankfully only cracked, not broken. His nose was broken. His hearing had mostly returned to normal, and while one eye was still swollen, he could see out of it. All in all, he'd been lucky. He hurt, there was no doubt about that, but he could be dead. He'd take the injuries over the alternative any day.

Tex was more than happy to agree to come back to the hospital if his leg got worse or if the pain got too bad. He knew better than anyone how important the health of his remaining leg was. He wasn't going to take any chances on losing it too. But he needed to be home. With his wife. In his own bed.

His entire world had been rocked in the last week, and as much as he loved and appreciated his friends, he needed some time with just Melody.

His daughters had both come to the hospital and cried when they'd seen him. Tex had even teared up a bit himself. Melody had held herself together, but he had a feeling when she was away from their daughters and friends, she'd let her true emotions show. And he was more than ready for that. He felt the same.

The painkillers coursing through his veins were making Tex feel a little floaty. Disconnected from what happened. But not so disconnected that he didn't want to hear everything that had happened since he and Melody had been snatched. How his friends found out what happened, what everyone had done to find him, *how* they'd found him, about Rook's accomplices, and what was happening with the police.

He didn't want to get into it in the hospital,

because there simply wasn't any length of time when he wasn't constantly being interrupted by nurses and doctors coming and going as they took blood, ran tests, and generally did their best to bring him back to his normal self.

There had been no sign of his prosthetic in the abandoned house, which sucked, because the one he'd been wearing when he was kidnapped was one of his favorites. But he had a few extra legs at home that he could use until he replaced his best one.

He and Melody were quiet as they sat in the back of Wolf's rental car, as he drove them back to his house. Tex gazed out the window while he held his wife's hand and marveled at how the places he saw on a daily basis seemed...new somehow. As if he was seeing them again for the first time.

The fact that Tex now had an idea of the feelings the people he helped experienced was both a blessing and a curse. He felt as if he could be more empathetic now toward both whoever he was looking for, as well as their loved ones. But knowing what they might be going through would also make his job a little bit harder, because it would put that much more pressure on him.

Tex sighed.

"You okay?" Melody asked for what seemed like the hundredth time.

"I am now that I'm back with you," he told her honestly.

Melody leaned her head against his shoulder and wrapped an arm around his biceps as she snuggled into him.

Tex had been able to get a sponge bath while in the hospital, but he longed for a proper shower. To rinse off the filth of that damn box once and for all. But first, he needed answers.

Wolf pulled into Tex's driveway and stopped.

Immediately, the car was surrounded by his friends. Everyone hovered, wanting to help in some way.

"Everyone back up," Melody ordered, as she exited and went around to Tex's side of the vehicle. Caroline got the wheelchair they'd rented at the hospital out of the back of the car and brought it around to Tex's side.

Expertly, as if he'd done the same thing thousands of times before, Tex transferred himself into the chair. It brought back memories of right after he'd lost his leg, when he'd been wheelchair bound before getting his prosthetic.

Melody got behind him to push the chair, the

only person Tex would now allow to do that for him, and they entered the house like a damn parade... everyone following behind Tex as if he was the leader of the band or something. It irritated him beyond measure, which was how he knew he had to find out the information he needed, then close himself in his bedroom with his wife for a few hours. He'd be better able to deal with everyone's concern after taking a nap while holding Melody.

She seemed to make everything better. Always had, even though Tex hadn't realized quite how much until right this moment.

He wheeled himself into the living room and transferred himself onto the couch. He'd be damned if he sat in the stupid wheelchair while he learned all the details about his kidnapping. Melody fussed a bit as she got a pillow to put under his leg, which he propped up on the coffee table in front of him.

"Where are Hope and Akilah?" he asked Melody, as everyone hovered around, getting settled.

"Amy has them. She took them from the hospital back to her house. She'll feed them, pack up their stuff, then bring them back here...giving you time to talk to everyone and get answers."

Again, his wife knew him so well. She was well aware he needed to talk about what happened, get all the details, without his kids being traumatized by overhearing any of it. He kissed her, letting his lips linger on hers. How he'd hit the jackpot with this woman, Tex had no idea, but he was even more thankful right this moment than he'd ever been.

Tex looked around the room. At Wolf sitting in the oversized chair with Caroline on his lap. At Baker leaning against the wall with his arms crossed, while his wife Jodelle worked with Annie to hand out bottles of water and soft drinks for those who wanted them. At Beth and Cade, who were next to Melody on the couch. It made for a tight fit with the four of them sitting there, but Tex wasn't complaining that his wife was plastered against his side.

Wolf's former teammates were scattered around the room. Mostly standing, as if too antsy to sit on the floor or the hearth of the fireplace.

The urge to say thank you again was on the tip of his tongue, but remembering Mozart's warning, he kept the words to himself. He'd find a way to thank everyone in this room one way or another. As well as everyone who wasn't physically there who'd also worked to find him...like Ryleigh and Rex. As well as those who'd donated money toward his ransom. If it took him the rest of his life, Tex would backtrack every donation and personally make sure the person who sent it knew how appreciated the gesture had been.

He'd have to be sneaky about it, because if he suddenly became the "thank you" man, people would freak.

That thought made him smile a little. Then he sobered.

"All right, lay it on me. Don't leave out a damn thing either. The good, bad, and ugly, I want it all," he ordered firmly. Turning to Melody, he said, "You first, Mel. What happened after you were pushed out of that fucking van?"

Seeing the cast on Melody's arm and the fading bruises had been difficult enough, but hearing first-hand what she'd gone through made Tex want to hurl. How she'd suffered abrasions all along her side. How terrified she'd been for those seconds before she got her hood off, pushed onto a busy road and thinking she was about to get run over. The moment she'd spotted that brick with the note wrapped around it, but was then forced to leave it as she walked to get help.

Tex told the group how he'd been beaten when he'd arrived at the house, but no one had taken his hood off until after they'd cut away his clothes and ordered him to remove his prosthetic. How he'd been made to hop into the box while his captors laughed.

"We're going to find them. All of them," Baker said, hatred in his tone.

"The cops are already on it," Truck said. "Rook sang like a canary, and I got most of the names before he...passed away."

Tex gazed at the large man and narrowed his eyes. He didn't need to know the details of what Truck had done to get the information about the other men who'd helped Rook. But he *did* need to know one thing. "Did he suffer?" he asked.

"Oh yeah. The asshole suffered."

"I should feel bad about that, knowing what he dealt with," Melody said quietly from Tex's side. "That he'd been going through the anguish of never knowing what happened to his wife...but that didn't give him the right to do what he did to you."

"And you," Tex insisted.

Melody shrugged. "A broken arm is nothing compared to what happened to you."

"We aren't going to compare horror stories," Tex said firmly. "You were traumatized just as I was."

She nodded in acquiescence.

"Tell me more about Asher Rook," Tex said,

looking at Beth. "What did you and Ryleigh find out about him?"

"Apparently, he tracked you down and asked for your help finding his wife, around the same time you were knee-deep looking for Kalee," Beth said.

Tex nodded. He remembered that time. He'd become almost as obsessed as Phantom with finding the woman who'd grabbed hold of his friend's heart and wouldn't let go. "I vaguely remember Rook now," he mused. "He didn't have much information, other than she disappeared while at a football game. I did contact the detective on the case up in Pittsburgh, and he told me he had a team of four men looking into videos from the stadium, and he had high hopes they'd be able to find something. It was his opinion that she'd disappeared on purpose. I guess Rook was abusive...something *he* didn't tell me, of course. The detective guessed she'd just had enough. I suspected going to the game was a ruse, and she got on a bus or something and got the hell out of town and away from him. Finding Kalee Solberg was much more important than tracking down an abused wife who had every right to get away from a man who was hurting her."

"I'd say you more than *vaguely* remember him," Benny said with a chuckle.

Tex shrugged. As he'd begun speaking about the missing woman, more and more of the details came back to him. "So…Rook took me hostage because he was pissed at me?" Tex asked the room in general.

"Pretty much," Truck said with a nod. "I asked him why he took Melody too, and he said because he wanted you to suffer, knowing your wife was hurt and you couldn't do a damn thing about it."

"He succeeded in that, damn him," Tex muttered.

"He learned enough from the video games he loved to play to make it seem like he was a professional hit man or something," Wolf said. "He hired people he'd made friends with online. Others like him, who spent hours playing those real-life simulation war games. It's scary how well they were able to execute their plan."

"Yeah, it was," Tex agreed, remembering how they'd beat on him every time he was dragged out of that box. "Where are these men now?"

"They'll be dealt with," Truck said, his voice hard.

That was enough for Tex. For once, he was going to let others deal with the people who'd kidnapped him and Melody. He needed to put this behind him. But he was going to find the SEAL who participated in his beating. That man was his to find and punish. No one tarnished the SEAL name. No one. "How'd you find me?" he asked, aiming the question at Beth.

She explained how Ryleigh had come up with the possible locations where he could be held, and how his friends had split up to search them.

"We were stretched a little thin, but I didn't want to wait for anyone else to fly out here," Wolf explained. "You should know that there were at least half a dozen teams that offered to do just that. The rest of Truck's team, Rocco and his SEALs, Trigger and his Deltas. Rex offered to send his Mountain Mercenaries, and I even had a call from Bull over in Indianapolis, who was about to get on a plane with his Silverstone team. Not only that, but I think every single person you've ever helped was more than willing to come out here as well. But I thought the last thing we needed—Melody needed—was dozens of people to play hostess for. Not that anyone would expect that, but we all know your wife, and she'd want to personally make sure each and every person who came was fed and aware of her gratitude."

Tex looked down at Melody. One of the many reasons he loved her was because of her huge heart. And he could totally see her trying to make sure everyone's belly was full and they were taken care of, instead of looking after herself.

"Anyway, as I was saying, we were running a little thin, but we all knew to immediately contact the others if we found something," Wolf told Tex. "And I put the rest of my guys on Melody."

"Wait—*on* her?" Tex asked, confused. "She wasn't here at home, waiting to see if you found me?"

An uneasy silence greeted his question.

Tex turned to his wife. "Mel?"

"It wasn't a huge deal. We were told that the money drop was supposed to take place at The Sugar Shack. You know, that abandoned factory? And I was the one who was supposed to take the money."

Tex felt as if his head was about to explode. He pinned an irate gaze on Wolf. "You let her go to a money drop? Are you *insane?*"

"It was obvious he wasn't going to be there," Beth piped in. "It's not as if she could actually get her hands on a billion dollars, much less lug it to a drop in cash. It wouldn't even fit in the SUV."

"We came back to the house as soon as we realized The Sugar Shack was deserted," Melody told him calmly.

Tex felt anything but calm, but he reminded himself that everything turned out all right in the end. Melody was fine, and he would be soon. He'd still never wanted to pace so much in his entire life. "I can't believe he asked for a billion dollars," he said, shaking his head. "He had to know getting that much money was impossible."

"Actually..." Abe started. "Last I heard, there was a billion and some change in the account Ryleigh set up to take donations."

Tex's eyes widened. "Say again?" He was aware people had donated money toward the ransom, but he hadn't known how much was raised.

"When people heard that you were in trouble, that the kidnapper demanded money, they were more than happy to donate. And to contact people who have more money than they can ever spend in one lifetime. You've touched so many people, Tex, they all wanted to give back in some way," Caroline explained. "And those you haven't helped, apparently wanted to make a donation in case they might need you and your skills in the future."

Tex couldn't believe what he was hearing. First that Rook had the balls to demand a billion dollars as a ransom, and second that it had actually been raised. It was going to take a hell of a long time to thank each and every person who'd donated. Longer than he'd anticipated.

"Anyway, I went to The Sugar Shack with some

duffel bags packed with towels, just in case he was there, but as we thought, the area was completely deserted. No sign of anyone," Melody explained. "Abe, Cookie, Benny, and Mozart were all with me. Checking the area out, making sure I was safe."

That was something. Tex trusted those men with his life. More importantly, with *Melody's* life.

He turned his gaze to Annie. "And you and Truck were tasked with checking out the house."

She nodded. "Truck went to the front and I went around back. I looked in the windows. One room was trashed, but the other had those blackout curtains over it. It was suspicious as hell. I thought the window being unlocked meant it was a trap, but then I saw that chair in the middle of the room and...that box." Her voice trembled slightly on the last two words.

Tex didn't like to think about the box he'd been kept in, but he was free. Wasn't in there anymore.

Annie went on to explain to everyone in the room how she'd texted Wolf, then gone in, picked the locks on the box, and gotten him out.

She sounded so matter-of-fact about how she'd picked him up as if he weighed no more than a child and gotten them both as far away from the house as possible.

"I know becoming a green beret wasn't easy," Tex said quietly. "I know you've been harassed and you've had to work twice as hard as everyone else to be able to take your place amongst the best of the best. But from where I'm sitting, there's no one else I would've wanted to free me from that hell. You did everything right, Annie, without hesitation. And don't think I missed how you protected me when we heard those shots fired. You're going to be an asset to any platoon you're in, and I have no doubt you'll rise up the ranks and be in charge of your own unit sooner rather than later."

Annie's eyes filled with tears, but she controlled them. "Thanks, Tex."

He looked around the room at his friends and felt extremely blessed. There had been many times in the past when he'd felt as if he was alone in what he did. Sitting in his basement, clicking away at his keyboard, no one to float ideas off of, running on his instincts and pure adrenaline when he found the evidence he needed to find whoever was missing.

But he wasn't alone. Not even close. The bank account with a billion freaking dollars in it, and the men and women in this room, proved just that, as did everyone sitting and standing in his living room.

He was sure he'd have more questions later, but

for the moment, Tex was done. It was suddenly difficult to keep his eyes open, and he needed to lie down, hold his wife, and count his blessings.

Looking around, he spoke slowly and clearly, wanting everyone in the room to truly hear what he was about to say. "Thank you. For being here. For protecting Melody, my kids, for doing what needed to be done to find me, for protecting me. It means the world to me."

"Oh shit, the world is ending, isn't it?" Cookie said under his breath. "Tex thanking people...who would've thought?"

Everyone chuckled. Even Tex's lips quirked upward in a grin.

"On that note, I'm going to go to my room and sleep. Don't interrupt me under any circumstances. Got it?"

"Yup."

"Of course."

"Wouldn't dream of it."

"You got it, boss."

"And when I wake up, I'm gonna go down to my basement and make sure you and Ryleigh didn't mess up my files," Tex grumbled, glancing at Beth.

She laughed.

"No one messed up anything," Cade said with a roll of his eyes.

"I'll text the names of the men who helped Rook," Truck told him. "They'll be dealt with, but I know you'll want their names anyway."

Damn straight he did. He nodded at Truck.

"I know you said you wanted to shower, but I think you should probably wait and do that in the morning," Melody said quietly.

"I feel fine," he insisted. Which was a lie. He felt like shit. His calf hurt—hell, his missing leg hurt—he had a headache, and he was exhausted. But no one needed to know that shit. Though, now that he thought about showering, he was relieved there was a built-in bench in the shower since he wouldn't be able to stand up to get himself clean. Which sucked.

"Come on, Iron Man," Melody said with a chuckle. "I could use a nap myself."

He figured as much. He doubted Mel had slept much while he'd been missing. He was more than happy to go straight to bed as long as she was joining him.

It was a damn ordeal to get back into the wheelchair and into his bedroom. Tex would be very glad when he had his leg back on and his calf healed so he could be more mobile.

"I'll entertain Hope and Akilah when they get back with Amy," Caroline said.

"And I'll make dinner," Benny volunteered.

Tex nodded at them, already looking forward to seeing what Benny came up with for everyone to eat. The man was a genius in the kitchen.

He was about to close the door to his bedroom when Annie spoke loudly from the living area. "I'm thinking you might be a little more open to wearing that fancy new tracker you've been pushing on me now, huh?"

The little shit.

She wasn't wrong. Tex had no doubt if he'd been wearing the prototype he'd invented, the one that was injected under the skin much like a dog or cat's microchip, he would've been found much sooner. Probably almost immediately.

"I will if you will!" he called back.

He heard Annie let out a whoop of delight before Melody shut the door. She also had a grin on her face. Without fuss, she helped Tex get into bed and immediately climbed in next to him. The second he had his arms around her, Tex felt himself relax completely for the first time.

He hadn't been embarrassed for Annie to see him without a stitch of clothing on. He hadn't been upset that he wasn't able to rescue himself. And he wasn't ashamed of the way he'd cried when he'd first laid eyes on Melody, and seen for himself that she was all right. A little banged up, but alive.

But here, in his home, his bed, his wife in his arms, Tex let himself feel all the emotions he'd bottled up for the last week. The fear, the uncertainty, the worry, the anger, the disbelief that he'd been fucking *kidnapped*. He cried as his wife held him as tightly as she could with her uninjured arm, crying right along with him.

Afterward, he felt better, but completely drained.

"Gonna sleep now," he warned her.

"Shhhhh. I've got you."

"I love you," Tex told her. "I'm proud of you for how strong you've been."

"I love you too. We have some pretty amazing friends."

"Yes, we do," Tex agreed.

The last thing he was fully aware of was how nice it was, the absolute silence of the room. He'd never take that kind of thing for granted again. Would never take *any* of his blessings for granted. His health, his family, his friends. He was a lucky man.

I hope you all loved this story that hit me hard and wouldn't let go. It was actually partially based on a true story I saw on TV once. A man was kidnapped south of the US border and kept for MONTHS while his family tried to work with the kidnappers to bring him home safe and sound. He was kept in a situation much like Tex was in this story, in a box, loud music playing, alone week after week. He was held for months, and then one day his kidnappers simply let him go. And he walked home. Battered, beaten, but alive. It inspired me and I thought…what if that happened to our Tex? Too bad the man in the real-live story didn't have a tracker. Or special forces friends. Or Annie.

There were so many characters in this story I can't really list them all, but if you're unfamiliar with them all, they came from, in no particular order, the following series:
SEAL of Protection, The Refuge, Badge of Honor, SEAL Team Hawaii, and *Delta Force Heroes.*

If you haven't read the story of how Tex and Melody met, you can find it here: *Protecting Melody.*

Also by Susan Stoker

SEAL of Protection Series
Protecting Caroline
Protecting Alabama
Protecting Fiona
Marrying Caroline (novella)
Protecting Summer
Protecting Cheyenne
Protecting Jessyka
Protecting Julie (novella)
Protecting Melody
Protecting the Future
Protecting Kiera (novella)
Protecting Dakota
Protecting Tex

SEAL of Protection: Alliance Series
Protecting Remi
Protecting Wren
Protecting Josie
Protecting Maggie (Apr 1, 2025)
Protecting Addison (May 6, 2025)
Protecting Kelli (Sept 2, 2025)
Protecting Bree (Jan 6, 2026)

Rescue Angels

Keeping Laryn (July 1, 2025)
Keeping Amanda (Nov 4, 2025)
Keeping Zita (Feb 10, 2026)
Keeping Penny (TBA)
Keeping Kara (TBA)
Keeping Jennifer (TBA)

Alpha Cove Series

The Soldier (Aug 12, 2025)
The Sailor (Mar 3, 2026)
The Pilot (Aug 4, 2026)
The Guardsman (TBA)

Eagle Point Search & Rescue

Searching for Lilly
Searching for Elsie
Searching for Bristol
Searching for Caryn
Searching for Finley
Searching for Heather
Searching for Khloe

The Refuge Series

Deserving Alaska
Deserving Henley

Deserving Reese
Deserving Cora
Deserving Lara
Deserving Maisy
Deserving Ryleigh

Delta Force Heroes Series

Rescuing Rayne
Rescuing Aimee (novella)
Rescuing Emily
Rescuing Harley
Marrying Emily
Rescuing Kassie
Rescuing Bryn
Rescuing Casey
Rescuing Sadie (novella)
Rescuing Wendy
Rescuing Mary
Rescuing Macie (novella)
Rescuing Annie

Delta Team Two Series

Shielding Gillian
Shielding Kinley
Shielding Aspen
Shielding Jayme (novella)

Shielding Riley

Shielding Devyn

Shielding Ember

Shielding Sierra

SEAL of Protection: Legacy Series

Securing Caite

Securing Brenae (novella)

Securing Sidney

Securing Piper

Securing Zoey

Securing Avery

Securing Kalee

Securing Jane

SEAL Team Hawaii Series

Finding Elodie

Finding Lexie

Finding Kenna

Finding Monica

Finding Carly

Finding Ashlyn

Finding Jodelle

Badge of Honor: Texas Heroes Series

Justice for Mackenzie

Justice for Mickie

Justice for Corrie

Justice for Laine (novella)

Shelter for Elizabeth

Justice for Boone

Shelter for Adeline

Shelter for Sophie

Justice for Erin

Justice for Milena

Shelter for Blythe

Justice for Hope

Shelter for Quinn

Shelter for Koren

Shelter for Penelope

Game of Chance Series

The Protector

The Royal

The Hero

The Lumberjack

Ace Security Series

Claiming Grace

Claiming Alexis

Claiming Bailey

Claiming Felicity

Claiming Sarah

<u>Mountain Mercenaries Series</u>
Defending Allye
Defending Chloe
Defending Morgan
Defending Harlow
Defending Everly
Defending Zara
Defending Raven

<u>Silverstone Series</u>
Trusting Skylar
Trusting Taylor
Trusting Molly
Trusting Cassidy

<u>Stand Alone</u>
Falling for the Delta
The Guardian Mist
Nature's Rift
A Princess for Cale
A Moment in Time - A Collection of Short Stories
Another Moment in Time - A Collection of Short Stories
A Third Moment in Time- A Collection of Short Stories
Lambert's Lady

Special Operations Fan Fiction
http://www.stokeraces.com/

Beyond Reality Series
Outback Hearts
Flaming Hearts
Frozen Hearts

Writing as Annie George:
Stepbrother Virgin (erotic novella)

ABOUT THE AUTHOR

New York Times, *USA Today*, #1 Amazon Bestseller, and *#1 Wall Street Journal* Bestselling Author, Susan Stoker has spent the last twenty-four years living in Missouri, California, Colorado, Indiana, Texas, and Tennessee and is currently living in the wilds of Maine. She's married to a retired Army man (and current firefighter/EMT) who now gets to follow *her* around the country.

She debuted her first series in 2014 and quickly followed that up with the SEAL of Protection Series, which solidified her love of writing and creating stories readers can get lost in.

If you enjoyed this book, or any book, please consider leaving a review. It's appreciated by authors more than you'll know.

www.stokeraces.com
www.AcesPress.com
susan@stokeraces.com